Horsefeathers

Horsefeathers!

Dandi Daley Mackall

CONCORDIA PUBLISHING HOUSE • SAINT LOUIS

Horsefeathers

Horsefeathers!
Horse Cents
Horse Whispers in the Air
A Horse of a Different Color
Horse Angels
Home Is Where Your Horse Is
Horsefeathers' Mystery
All the King's Horses

Published by Concordia Publishing House
3558 S. Jefferson Avenue, St. Louis, MO 63118-3968

Interest level: ages 12–16

Text copyright © 2000 Dandi Daley Mackall

Manufactured in the United States of America

Library of Congress Cataloging-in-Publication Data

Mackall, Dandi Daley.
     Horsefeathers! /Dandi Daley Mackall.
        p. cm.—(Horsefeathers)
     Summary: Eighth-grader Scoop lives with her aunt and grandfather on a horse farm they can barely maintain, but by trusting God and befriending a mysterious and wealthy new neighbor, Scoop finds a way to keep both the farm and her beloved horse Orphan.
     ISBN 0-570-07006-6
     [1. Horses—Fiction. 2. Mistaken identity—Fiction. 3. Orphans—Fiction. 4. Christian life—Fiction.] I. Title
PZ7.M1905 Ht   2000
[Fic]—dc21   00-012222

    6   7   8   9   10   11   10   09   08   07   06   05

To God, who created horses, and to all the horses

who have given me so much: Sugar, Misty,

Towaco, Rocket, Angel, Ash Bill, Butch, Cindy,

Lancer, Moby, Cheyenne, and those to come.

1

"Stephen Dalton, you touch that horse and you're dead!" I screamed.

Stephen's hand flew off the tailgate of the two-horse trailer. The ramp crashed to the ground, setting off the bay inside. The horse kicked and let out a high-pitched whinny that froze my soul.

"Mind your own business, Scoop!" Stephen yelled back. But he let the twitch fall to his side and shuffled farther away from the bay.

From where I sat bareback on Orphan, 100 feet from the rocking trailer, I could smell the salt sweat of fear—Stephen's, the bay's, mine.

"Scoop," Maggie pleaded, urging me from the back of her old white mare. "You can't let them use the twitch!"

Ray sat cross-legged in the tall grass, his long neck craning for a better view. "Why?" he asked in that easygoing drawl that makes each word last a long time. "What's a twitch?"

I pointed to the wooden bat in Stephen's hand. A loop of rope was tied through a hole in one end. "That loop fits over the horse's tender upper lip. Then they twist the bat part until the poor horse can't think of anything except the pain. I've seen Stephen's dad twitch horses to load at Dalton Stables. If one gets balky, they twitch him and break his spirit."

A convoy of Mayflower moving trucks bounced up the long drive, looking like a giant, disjointed green snake. They weren't going to help matters.

"Why wouldn't the horse just come out?" Ray asked. "He can't like it in there."

"He wants out," I said, feeling as if I were the one trapped. "But he doesn't know if *outside* will be any better than inside. He can't figure out where he belongs." I understood—that's how I feel half the time myself.

The bay snorted and let out a high-pitched squeal that even made Maggie's old mare look up. "He'll hurt himself!" Maggie cried.

Orphan picked up the tension and side-stepped. "Easy, girl," I murmured, stroking her sleek, black neck. It felt warm from the sun. I'd ridden over bareback, using Orphan's halter and lead as a bridle. If she decided to take off, I wouldn't have much to say about it without a bit on my side.

Thwack! Thwack! Thwack! The bay pawed the trailer floor. Stephen ran his fingers through his red hair and backed off. A burly man with shaggy brown hair climbed out of the cab and peeked inside the trailer.

"Clydesdale," I whispered to Maggie. That's what I imagined the man would have been if he'd been a horse. Twigs cracked under his big boots as he lumbered to the back of the trailer. It was already summer hot, with no breeze at all, as if God had skipped spring.

"Let's try pulling him out," said the Clydesdale man, grabbing the long, wavy black tail.

But the bay didn't give him a chance. He reared and snorted and kicked. My heart pounded so loud in my ears I couldn't hear what Stephen was saying. Behind us, moving vans ground to a stop.

A woman in a pale blue business suit stormed out of the house. She must have gotten there before we did. I'd never seen her before. "What's wrong here?" she shouted, charging the Clydesdale man. She was what Maggie calls petite instead of little. I'd call her classy, spirited like an Arabian mare.

Her glare stunned the Clydesdale man. "Uh ... doesn't want to come out," he said.

"No kidding," Ray muttered. He leaned back on his elbows and crossed his long legs at the ankles.

The woman grabbed the twitch out of Stephen's hand and shoved it at the Clydesdale man. "You've got a twitch. Use it!" She turned and stomped back inside, slamming the screen door behind her.

I couldn't let it happen. The situation wasn't the horse's fault. I slid off Orphan and threw the lead rope over to Ray. It slapped him on the arm.

"Scoop!" he cried. "What am I supposed to do with this?"

"Hold her," I said, making eye contact with Orphan that told her to stay put.

"Yea!" Maggie hollered. "Go Scoop!" She bounced in her saddle and waved her arm over her head as if she had a lasso to throw.

I ran up and blocked the Clydesdale man's path. Sweat dripped from his forehead. "Please don't twitch him," I said.

Stephen started to say something, but I stared him into silence.

"Have to," said the man. Up close he was bigger than I'd thought when I was looking on from Orphan's back. I'm 5'4", 110 pounds, and the man was at least a foot taller and twice as heavy. But he had a kindness in his eyes—like a Clydesdale.

"Truth is," he said, "I don't cotton much to twitching horses either. But that blamed horse won't come out. I thought we'd never get him *in* the trailer back in Kentucky." He stepped around me.

I raced around in front of him. "Will you let me try? Please? Just let me try." Inside I was talking to God. Dotty, the aunt I live with, would have said God was caring more about this bay than I was.

The Clydesdale man shook his head.

"She can talk a horse into anything!" Maggie yelled over. She was standing up in the metal stirrups of her English saddle, while her mare grazed as if none of this was any of her business.

"You ought to let her try," Ray hollered. "And quick! I don't know how long I can hold this horse of hers."

I grinned at Ray. He's okay for a non-horselover.

I could tell the man wanted to let me do it. "I don't know," he said, wiping sweat from his forehead. "You might get hurt."

"Sarah Coop? Scoop? Hurt by a fellow horse? Never!" Maggie said in her dramatic actress voice. "Neh-vah!"

A thump came from the trailer. Stephen scurried behind a twisted oak tree. The whole trailer jerked. That horse was going to kill himself if I didn't do something. "I'm going in with him, okay?" I said.

The man pressed his lips together and puffed out his cheeks. "Okay, but come out if it looks dangerous!" He handed me the twitch.

I threw it in the dirt and stepped into the empty side of the trailer. "Hey, boy," I said in a low voice, moving closer an inch at a time.

9

"Humans. Can't trust them, can we."

When I reached the bay's head, I sensed him stiffen. He pawed the trailer floor. Even lathered in sweat and foam, he was beautiful, maybe a hand—4 inches—taller than Orphan, which would put him at 16.2 or better. I could tell he had perfect confirmation—rounded rump, straight legs set just far enough apart for healthy organs.

He thrust his head around to see me. His eyes were wide with fright, but set well on the sides of an intelligent head.

"You're a looker," I murmured. I didn't stare at him because horses don't like that. Already I could see by the worry lines at his eyes that this wasn't his first battle. Little scars on his muzzle showed he'd been twitched before.

"What's taking you so long?" Stephen hollered through the window, startling the bay. The horse shook his head, his long, black mane waving like a flag on a windy day.

Horsefeathers! I thought. I couldn't answer because I didn't want to yell. I just hoped Maggie would take care of Stephen. "Easy, boy," I said. "Don't mind Stephen Dalton. Between you and me, he's not worth it."

When the bay turned toward me this time, he widened his nostrils and moved his muzzle inches from my face. I held still. This was my chance. Gently, I blew into his nostrils. It's the way horses introduce themselves. They snort in each other's faces, exchanging and accepting each other's smell. We didn't move. It was as if we were the only two creatures on earth, locked together in some cave. Then the bay snorted back at me. And I was in.

I snorted once more. The gelding's ears flicked up and back, like antennae. I felt his warm breath on my eyelids. I inched my hand where he could see it, then scratched his chin, his jaw, then high on his neck. He was nothing but a big sweetie.

"What say you and me get out of this fire-trap?" I lifted the lead rope and slid it down low, next to his foreleg. Then I walked backwards, tugging gently, then letting up, then tugging again. "Come on. I want you to meet Orphan. She's going to love you." The ramp rattled under his hooves. He stopped, then started again.

Slowly, a step at a time, he backed onto the ramp. I kept chattering. "You're probably booked in at Dalton Stables, ritziest place in town, although I have to warn you: They don't believe in horsing around there."

Three quick steps, and he was down. Applause broke all around us—Ray, Maggie, the moving men. I felt my face grow hot.

The Clydesdale man took the lead from me. "Nice job, kid," he said.

"We'll take it from here." Stephen pushed me aside.

"Scoop!" Ray called. "Come get your horse! I think she's jealous." Orphan was straining at her lead. She'd pulled Ray up off the lawn. Good ol' Ray. He'd just come to see if the new people had kids our age—14 or 15. He hadn't bargained for this.

Beside Orphan, Maggie now sat side-saddle on her horse, who was still grazing ... *with* her bridle on. Maggie figured you can't teach a 23-year-old horse new tricks—even though hers knew more real tricks than any horse I'd ever run across.

"I knew you'd do it!" Maggie said. This week Maggie, or Margaret Brown, was calling herself Maggie Green. She smoothed her hair under her green-silk jockey's cap. Next to her horse's white satiny coat, Maggie's clear, black complexion seemed even darker. In black jodhpurs and a green, silk shirt, she looked like she belonged in the movies, which is where she plans to end up.

I hugged Orphan and rubbed my face on the white blaze that runs the length of her head. She smelled better than horse, which is as good as it gets. Orphan rubbed her velvety muzzle against my cheek in a horse kiss.

I grabbed a fistful of mane and swung myself up on her broad back. Leaning forward, I wrapped my arms around her neck and whispered, "You know I love you best. You'll always be my Orphan." I'd always taken care of her, and nobody else had ever ridden her. I just hadn't saved up enough money to buy her from Grandad and make it official.

I was feeling pretty good, soaking up the sun's rays and listening to crows caw high in the branches of a walnut tree. But I should have known it wouldn't last.

"Sarah Coop! Scoop!" Stephen called, walking back to us. "I've got something to tell you."

Horsefeathers! I didn't lift my head from Orphan's neck. All I could see were Stephen's boots marching toward me. Stephen Dalton, who never rides his horse unless he's showing or practicing for a horse show, had on expensive English riding boots anyway. His leather heels squirted gravel as he stepped in so close I could see his beady eyes. And from the smug look on his pale, milky face, I knew whatever he had to tell me, I wasn't going to like it one bit.

2

"What is it, Stephen?" I asked, trying not to give him the satisfaction of seeing me squirm.

He stopped just in front of Orphan and frowned up at me, shielding his eyes with one hand. He has the longest fingers and cleanest fingernails I've ever seen. "I really shouldn't tell you," he said, drawing out each word, rising up on his toes and back down, up and down, his heels grinding into grass. "Promised Dad I wouldn't."

That was so like him. "Then you better not," I said. But what I felt like doing was ripping it out of him with my bare hands.

"I'll give you a hint. *Horsefeathers!*" He said it in a raspy, old man's voice, which I knew was supposed to be Jared Coop's, Stephen's grandfather—mine too, kind of.

I had only two things in common with the old man. The first was Orphan, officially Grandad's horse until I could come up with the money to buy her. And the second was the word "horsefeathers," just about the only thing he'd passed along to his son, who managed to leave it with me. "Horsefeathers yourself, Stephen," I said, pulling myself up straight on Orphan's back.

Actually, *horsefeathers* is one of the only things I can remember about the only dad I can remember. He'd drag home from the bottle plant, and if Mom didn't have supper on the table, he'd say, "Horsefeathers, Emma! A man works hard all day." Then she'd go in to work the night shift. But that was before the accident.

Grandad Coop didn't want anything to do with me or my aunt, Dotty. But since he really owned Orphan, and Orphan's barn, I usually tried to make nice or stay out of his way. I couldn't imagine why Stephen thought I'd give a hoot about his big secret. "Go peddle your secrets somewhere else," I said.

Stephen moved closer, like he wanted to whisper something more to me. But Orphan smelled something she didn't like. She pranced in place and laid her ears back flat.

"Keep that orange nag under control!" Stephen whined, jerking out of the way.

Orphan did have an orange tint to her black coat already. "She's not orange," I muttered. "It's a healthy sunburn from living outside in the fresh air instead of being cooped up in a stable like your poor horses." I stroked Orphan's warm neck under her mane. People who show or raise black horses for money keep them out of the sun. I knew enough to get the insult.

"Stephen!" Ralph Dalton's scream reached across the lawn like fingernails on a blackboard. "Get over here!"

"Put a large sock in it, Dad!" Stephen bellowed, smirking at me like I should be impressed or something. Then he cupped one hand to his mouth and whispered up to me: "Grandfather Coop—"

"You'll ... sorry ... business ... mother if ... now!"

I couldn't make out what his dad was shouting, but Stephen got enough of it to look worried. "I'll be going now," he said, trotting over to his dad. "Scoop, don't forget—*horsefeathers*." He used that old man voice again. "Go over there and ask Grandfather what's new."

I didn't like the gleam in Stephen's eye. Part of me wanted to ride over and see Grandad right then. But the other part of me didn't want to leave—especially since that's what Stephen wanted me to do. I decided to drop in on Grandad when I took Orphan back.

Another fleet of moving vans thundered up the long driveway. "Better look out, Stephen!" I called after him. "You may not be the richest kid in town anymore." I knew that would get him where it hurt.

"I guess the show's over," Maggie said, tugging at her horse's reins. A wad of long grass stuck out of the mare's mouth, like a green mustache. "I promised Jen I'd go riding with her, then hit the library."

Maggie held her right arm straight up from her side, as if she were preparing to take a bow. Instead, her gleaming white horse curled her left front leg and bent her head in a deep bow. "Exit stage left," Maggie said. She stuck on her riding helmet and trotted off, posting.

For a second—just a second—I felt a dull pang and wondered why Jen and Maggie hadn't asked me along. But it really didn't matter. I called after her, "Be careful on that wild Paint! Tell Jen to work her on the lunge line before she rides!"

One by one, more vans pulled up on the lawn. Four moving men with bulging arm muscles had to thread through shagbark hickories to get up to the big porch. The trees already had most of their leaves and stretched their branches all across the lawn, spotting the ground with shadows.

From Orphan's back I could read the labels on top of the boxes that littered the overgrown yard. This was one filthy rich family moving in.

Ray stretched his long legs and sat up in the grass where he'd been playing possum. He's one of the few people I don't feel uncomfortable around. If he were a horse, he'd be a Tennessee Walking Horse, so easygoing you'd hardly know he was moving.

"Work that Indian sixth sense, Scoop," Ray said. "What's the family like?" Ray was convinced I came from pure Indian ancestry. I don't have a clue about my biological parents, but I kind of like Ray's theory. I usually wear my hair in a thick, brown braid that almost reaches my waist. And although I know my skin is this dark from the sun, Ray could still be right.

"Ray," I said, "it's just horse sense. And I keep telling you I'm not as good at figuring out people as I am horses." Still, I didn't want to let him down.

I squeezed my thighs into Orphan's soft sides and moved to a spot about a horse-tail length from the porch.

Two movers were wrestling a huge crate up the steps. Two more climbed the metal ramp into the truck.

"All right," I said to Ray. "Our new neighbors are the Buckinghams." That was easy since I'd read it off a bunch of boxes. "For openers, they're rich." That was easy too. The Martin house, all stone and elegance, looked like it belonged in England or Scotland. It was the most expensive house in the county.

"And?" Ray urged.

"The mother's a lawyer," I said, satisfied to see his surprise. I was pretty sure about the lawyer part because of all the boxes marked *law books* and *study* and *library*. The mother part was a gamble. I'd heard the movers say, "Mrs. Buckingham said this," and "Mrs. Buckingham said that." And when she stormed out of the house in her blue suit, she looked like a lawyer.

By now millions of boxes and crates littered the lawn. The biggest stacks, right in front of us, read *Carla's Room* or *Carl's Room*. I couldn't imagine what two kids could do with all that stuff. Their room—or rooms—in their old house must have been giant. Four boxes on the porch were marked *Carla's 8th grade*, and two others had *Carl's 8th grade*.

"Give me the scoop, Scoop," Ray demanded. He raised bushy eyebrows at me and locked my gaze with his puppy-brown eyes.

"Two kids," I announced confidently. "One boy, one girl. Twins." It hadn't been that hard to figure out. Why else would somebody name their kids Carl and Carla? I wondered if they both loved horses. I could imagine long rides with Carla and her incredible bay gelding.

"Twins? You're good, Scoop," Ray said. "How old?"

"I'm pretty sure the twins are going into ninth grade like us." In two weeks when school would be over, I knew Dotty would pack up my school junk in a box marked *8th grade* too. Only my box would only be about half as big as one of theirs.

"I can't wait to meet them," I said. Maybe I could ride with Carla—or with both of them—every day after school, especially when Maggie had play practice or ballet or music lessons.

After a while Ray got up and headed for his blue trail bike, which leaned against an oak tree. "Tell B.C. hey for me, will you, Scoop?" he said.

B.C. is short for "Bottle Cap," who happens to be named Benjamin Coop. My brother, born to my folks after they adopted me, would be finishing third grade—if they let him graduate. B.C. never quite got over losing Mom and Dad, even though he doesn't remember having them. Ray is one of the few kids who understands B.C. and his moods. "Thanks, Ray!" I called after him.

Without turning around, Ray waved from his bike. Then he clasped his hands behind his neck, elbows sticking out, and coasted down the lane.

I hung around and watched the emergence of 24 tables, seven beds, an army of chairs, and I don't know how many boxes marked *FRAGILE*. I was just about to go when I caught sight of something I'll never forget.

I think I smelled the leather before I saw the first bridle. It had a scent like cooked cherries and pine bark. Two moving men carrying a huge, wooden sawhorse stumbled down the ramp of one of the Mayflower trucks. On the sawhorse hung six saddles and twice as many bridles. Behind those, two more movers carried a second sawhorse, this one covered with English saddles, halters, ropes, and more bridles. I closed my eyes and breathed deeply, imagining this must be what heaven smells like.

I dropped to the ground, wrapped Orphan's rope around a branch, and moved in closer. That's when I spotted one of the bridles on the ground. It had probably fallen off when they stepped from the ramp. I picked up the bridle and fingered the snaffle bit and red band at the forepiece.

"I'll take that!" someone yelled. She grabbed the bridle out of my hands. At the same time, she stumbled over one of the boxes and sprawled at Orphan's feet. Her shiny black hair covered her face, but I could see she looked just like her lawyer mom. One yellow sandal flew in the air. And her dress twisted around her as she struggled to get up.

I couldn't help but laugh. "You okay?"

She didn't answer. I wondered why anyone would wear a dress when she didn't have to. And how could anybody who looked like a prom queen have a bridle like this? Life was so unfair.

I reached down to untangle the reins of the bridle for her. She jerked it away from me and scrambled up on her own.

I hadn't done anything, but I felt guilty anyway and probably looked guilty too. I used to take things, to shoplift stuff. I don't anymore. But certain people—like Stephen and my grandfather—never let me forget it.

"Look," I said. "I was just picking up your bridle. It was on the ground, and—"

But she had already turned away, rumpled and fuming. Clutching the bridle to her, she stomped up the porch steps. I stared after her, wondering if Stephen had already gotten to her, if he could have told her about my shoplifting days. He'd told everybody else.

"Wait!" I protested, jogging after her, up the steps and onto the front porch. "I'm your neighbor, Sarah Coop. S. Coop. Scoop. We're going to be classmates. Your horse—"

But she acted as if she hadn't heard a word I'd said. The door slammed in my face, a big slam followed by little ones until the screen door was still ... and she was gone, disappeared into the darkness of the house.

"So that's Carla," I deduced out loud. I hopped off the porch, knocking over one of the sawhorses. No way I'd pick it up.

I jumped on Orphan, all my visions of riding partners and horse-loving neighbors evaporating. All I wanted to do was get as far away as possible from "Buckingham Palace."

Horsefeathers.

3

I couldn't get off the Buckingham royal estate
fast enough—one more place I didn't belong.
Orphan broke to a rolling canter across the pasture. It was exactly what I wanted, even though
I hadn't guided her. She'd read my heart. That's
how I think God works. I can't talk to God
smooth and natural like Dotty does. But He
senses what I mean anyway. He reads my heart.

We'd just reached the roadside when
Orphan started limping. I hopped off and
stroked her right forefoot. My chest hurt, imagining that she could be in any kind of pain.
"What's the matter, Orphan?" I asked her.

Most people will tell you horses can't understand English. But Orphan does. And I understand her—about a hundred times better than I
understand people. She craned her head around,
nuzzling my arm as I pulled burrs out of her fet-
lock. Slowly, I ran my fingers down her white-
stockinged leg, feeling the pastern, or ankle, for
cuts or bumps.

I leaned into Orphan and lifted her hoof. Right away I spotted the trouble. A rock had pushed into the frog of her underhoof. That's the soft middle part, shaped like a V. I scratched at it with my bare hands, wishing I didn't bite my nails so I could pinch the rock out.

"What's prob'em?" The voice was thin and kind of hard to understand. I dropped Orphan's hoof. A kid just a little taller than me stood at my elbow. He wore sweatpants, a baggy black sweatshirt, and a Cleveland Indians baseball cap turned backwards. The guy looked kind of familiar.

I stared at him until it clicked. "You're Carl," I said. He looked enough like Carla to be a twin—Latin or Spanish—small-boned, big, brown eyes. Besides, I knew every kid in town. So it didn't take much horse sense, Indian or not, to put the pieces together.

"Throw a shoe?" he asked, his voice still sounding weird. He moved around where he could see. Then he patted Orphan high on the neck, her favorite spot.

"She didn't throw a shoe," I said gruffly. Orphan didn't throw a shoe because she didn't wear horseshoes. She didn't need or want shoes, not that I could have afforded them anyway. "My horse picked up a rock." I really wished he'd just go back to Buckingham Palace where he belonged.

"We better get it out." Listening to Carl was

like deciphering a code. He left off the endings of words. It took a few seconds for my brain to fill in the missing sounds and get his meaning. Carl looked around, then ran to the side of the road and came back with a short stick.

"I'll do it," I said, grabbing the stick from him. I guess I wasn't being my nicest because of his sister. I tried to hold Orphan's hoof up with one hand and dig out the rock with the other. But Orphan shifted her weight and made me drop the stick.

"Want me to hold her halter?" Carl asked.

I nodded and picked up the stick. I glanced at Carl while I worked on the rock. He was the spitting image of his sister. But I guess that's why they call them twins. In less than a minute I had the rock out.

Carl patted Orphan on her favorite spot again. "There you go. That's a good girl. You won't limp now." It came out: *You wone limb now.* I remembered a kid in kindergarten who talked like that, but he outgrew it.

I began feeling guilty for acting unfriendly. It wasn't Carl's fault that his twin was so crabby. "Thanks," I said. "My name's Scoop. Actually Sarah Coop. But they call me Scoop."

He didn't look up. "What's your horse's name?"

"Orphan. But I don't own her exactly. I take care of her for my grandad. He owns the barn and pastures over there." I pointed across the field that now probably belonged to the Buckinghams. Nobody had planted crops there for several years, so the grass grew thick as shag carpet, and clover sprouted everywhere, along with briars and burrs.

"My grandad's land runs that way," I said, moving my arm toward the east, "up next to Dalton Stables, where your horse is. The Daltons have been trying to buy out Grandad Coop for years. I'm saving up to buy Orphan official like though." I didn't add that I still had less than $100.

We fell to walking together, with Orphan setting the pace. "Why did you name her Orphan?" he asked.

Before I knew it I was spilling the whole story. "Orphan was the horse nobody wanted, like me. Nobody wanted me until I was three. That's when I got adopted. Anyway, Old Jared Coop, my new dad's dad, owned this horse farm. He bred nothing but purebred quarter horses for showing.

"All but Orphan. Orphan was an accident. One of the mares broke loose and found herself a stallion. We were never positive which stallion. They say my grandfather nearly exploded."

Stephen has always called Orphan a mongrel just because she doesn't have papers. I waited for Carl to say something snotty, but he didn't.

"Anyway," I went on, "when Orphan was born, her mother died. That sure didn't make Grandad like Orphan any better." I stroked Orphan's shoulder as we walked. A tractor hummed from a distant field. Orphan's hooves beat a steady clip, clop, clip, clop. Sometimes I think it's the best music God invented.

Carl said, "That's why she's strong like a quarter horse, but graceful like a saddle horse, or maybe an Arabian. I thought she might be a Morgan."

I was getting used to the soft, mushy way his words came out, like *quar hor* and *sal hor*. It made me think of the fog that hangs over the pasture in the morning, making everything look fuzzy, as though the edges had worn off.

"I was three when they adopted me," I said, continuing the story. "I still hadn't said my first word. Not the brightest star in the sky, Grandad says. Anyway, my new dad and mom took me to the farm—my Aunt Dotty says to show me off. None of the Coop mares would nurse the scrawny, black foal that didn't belong. She was lying on her side breathing funny, and Grandad Coop couldn't get her to bottle feed. I took the bottle out of his hand and lay down beside the filly and fed her.

"When they tried to take me home, I put up such a fit, they had to let me sleep in the barn. Finally Mom grabbed a few horse blankets and stayed with me, huddled in the hay all night." I couldn't imagine that now. It made me wonder if it had really happened then.

Sometimes I think I can actually remember that day, the green, scratchy horse blanket, my mom dressed in green jeans and a checkered shirt, her breath on my neck as we squeezed together and scooched our shapes in the hay. But it's probably just Dotty's stories I remember.

I wiped sweat from my forehead and coughed. "In the morning the filly, black as night except for a narrow white blaze and four white stockings, was standing. And I was talking."

"And that's why you call her Orphan?" Carl asked.

"Not exactly," I said. "Stephen Dalton and his dad had come to the barn. Stephen's mom and my dad were sister and brother. Stephen was my age, but he'd been talking for a year already. When he spotted me, he pointed and sang out, 'Orphan, orphan!'

"I was so dumb, I guess I thought he was calling the filly. Dotty says I kissed the foal on her blaze and said plain as day, 'Orphan.' Nobody ever bothered to name her anything else. Two years ago I almost had enough to make Grandad Coop an offer he wouldn't laugh at. But something came up."

What had come up was B.C. He had started

coloring with black Crayolas on our walls, our floors, and on himself. We had to pay for some psychologist to talk him out of it. It took more money than any of us had saved up. Dotty worked extra hours at the Hy-Klas grocery store, and I forked over my horse bank.

"Do your parents ride?" Carl asked.

I felt a lump swell in my throat—the same lump that hadn't gone away in seven years. I looked down at Orphan's hooves striking the ground in rhythm. "They're dead. They were killed in an accident at the bottle plant."

Carl didn't say anything for a minute or two. Orphan's hooves kept banging out the beat. "I'm sorry," he said at last. "Who takes care of you?"

"My aunt. But she doesn't make us call her *Aunt*. She's just Dotty. She came to stay with my brother and me after the accident and she never left."

We'd reached the lane to Orphan's barn. Suddenly I felt really stupid for talking so much.

Carl bent down and lifted Orphan's hoof again. "You don't shoe her? Her hooves are so healthy."

I grinned. Carl's horses had probably been stabled their whole lives. "That's why they're healthy," I said. "I keep Orphan's hooves trimmed. But as long as we ride in the pastures or stay on trails or keep to the side of the road,

29

going shoeless is the best thing for hooves. Someday I'm going to run my own stable. But the horses won't be locked up like at Dalton Stables. They'll run free—barefoot bosses."

Carl set down Orphan's foot. When he stood up, something flopped from behind his right ear. It looked like a plastic tube with a bean on the end. I must have stared at it because Carl shoved the bean part back behind his ear. "Hearing aid," he explained.

"Horsefeathers. I'm sorry. I mean, I didn't know you couldn't ... . " Then I realized I was practically yelling.

"You don't need to shout," Carl said softly. "I'm not deaf. They call it *hearing impaired*."

I didn't know what to say. So I lowered my voice and changed the subject. "You're good with horses. Is the bay yours?"

He didn't say anything. A plover circled above us, shrieking to protect her nest. Crows cawed from the maple tree up the hill. I could hear grasshoppers jumping in the dry ditch. I wondered if Carl heard any of it.

"We used to have lots of horses," Carl said. "Mother believes in winning. Lots of horse shows in Kentucky. But we just brought Buckingham's British Pride with us. He's the best of the lot."

"He's beautiful," I said. "Is he Carla's then?"

He kicked the gravel, and I sensed something was wrong. I changed the subject again. "Is your mom a lawyer?"

"Both of my parents are lawyers," he said. "Dad's an international attorney, so he's gone most of the time."

I'd been right about the lawyer part, even though I'd missed the second one. I couldn't wait to tell Ray. "Are you finishing out eighth grade too?"

He nodded.

Right again. "If you get to choose homeroom teachers, try to get The Gopher."

Carl shook his head and tapped his hearing aid with the palm of his hand. "Sorry, Scoop. I thought you said I might get a gopher."

"I did. Mrs. Gopher. She got married on Groundhog's Day to George Gopher. No kidding."

"Did they see their shadow at the wedding?" he asked, grinning.

I laughed. "Anyway, that's where Ray and Maggie and I are. And Jen too."

Carl's smile disappeared. He kicked at the gravel.

Horsefeathers. I hadn't even thought about the fact that he was a boy and I was a girl. That was just one more way I didn't fit in. I hoped he wouldn't be like Ray and act like he didn't know me when we were at school. Boys are even harder to understand than regular people.

Carl turned to go.

"See you Monday, Carl!" I called after him, an uneasy feeling creeping into my veins. "Or tomorrow? We go to the church across from the Hy-Klas grocery store."

Carl kept going. Then, halfway up the hill, he turned to face me. "If you don't see me at school," he said, walking up the hill backwards, stumbling, " ... I'll meet you and Orphan after school. Come to my backyard."

"Sure," I called. "But why wouldn't I see you? Our school's not that big—"

But Carl was already running away. I thought about running after him, but something told me not to. It had to be over 80 degrees out, but I felt myself shiver. It might have been my imagination, but I think Orphan felt it too. She pawed the dirt.

Horsefeathers, I thought, pulling myself together. What was I worried about? Things were definitely looking up. I'd check in on Grandad Coop and get Stephen off my back. Then tomorrow, with any luck, Carl might even end up in my homeroom ... and Carla might not.

I turned Orphan loose in Grandad Coop's front pasture. She trotted straight to her rolling corner, the only spot in the pasture she didn't graze. I watched her buckle her knees and plop down in the bare dirt. She rolled to her side and kicked her legs straight out, twisting to scratch her back. With no effort at all, she rolled on her back, scratched, then went all the way over. Snorting playfully, she rolled back the other way.

"Go again, Orphan! You're not quite dirty enough!" I hollered, knowing that good old-fashioned dirt works a hundred times better than a cooling blanket for regulating body temperature and cooling a horse down safely.

The Coop Farm had everything a horse could want—a good-sized pond for swimming, a creek in the far pasture, and a barn big enough to house 30 horses, which it had in its day. I kept the door to Orphan's stall open so she could go inside whenever she wanted, which was almost never.

The barn felt empty as I walked through to Punch and Judy's paddock. The pair of 2-year-olds, the only horses Grandad had left, were destined to be champion quarter horses. When I got close, Judy nickered at me, and they both came running.

"Hi, girls," I called. I'd mucked their stalls, picked their hooves, and brushed them in the morning when I'd let them out. But Grandad made me stable them in the evenings. "Sorry, guys. Prison time." They followed me in, and I checked them over and fed them.

I hurried through the rest of the chores so I could still have time to drop in on Grandad Coop. In the back of my head I heard Stephen's dumb impersonation: *Horsefeathers.* I pulled down some hay to keep the girls entertained, then ran across the yard to Grandad's house, the same old two-story farmhouse he and his wife had built when they started up.

I practiced what I'd say: "Long time no see, Grandad." "Your grandson made fun of you today." "Horsefeathers, I see you're as crabby as ever."

Grandad Coop had never forgiven my dad for marrying young and leaving the farm. I guess Dotty and I were the only ones left to take it out on.

"Scoop! Scoop!" Maggie Brown came galloping up on her white horse Moby, named after

Moby Dick, the great white whale. Maggie had changed to a Western saddle, and now wore a green shirt with white fringe that matched her cowboy hat. Moby is in such great shape she didn't have a lick of sweat on her.

I met her in the driveway. "What's up, Maggie?"

"You have to help, Scoop!" she said, dramatic as usual. "Jen's horse jumped the fence, and they can't catch her."

"We better hurry," I said, climbing up on Moby, behind Maggie. "Dotty might be home late, and I don't want to leave B.C. alone too long."

Moby took off like a 3-year-old, and I had to tighten my leg grip to hang on.

Jen's mom, Mrs. Zucker, waved to us from her front porch, where she sat rocking the triplets. The Zucker family always looked like a herd of mustangs running wild. Two dogs barked from the porch step, and half a dozen cats hissed, fighting over a bowl of milk by the side of the house.

"There's Travis," Maggie whispered, sighing deeply. "He's so cute!"

Travis, Jen's older brother, would have made a terrific Palomino stallion, stately and well-muscled. All the Zuckers are blond and blue-eyed, except for Mr. Zucker, who's bald, claiming he pulled out his hair when the triplets were born.

Travis was out in the field with Jen and Mr. Zucker.

Cheyenne raced along the fence, her tail held high. She's a beautiful sorrel-and-white Paint, a Tobiano, with solid quarter-horse lines and a gorgeous head. She trotted toward Jen a few steps, snorted, then took off again. I slid off Moby and crossed the pasture, ducking under the fence Cheyenne must have jumped.

"Scoop's here!" Travis yelled, as soon as he saw me. He flashed me his smile and walked up to meet me mid-field. "I give up on the beast," he said, squinting because of the setting sun at my back. "We've been out here for over an hour, Scoop!"

Jen and Mr. Zucker came panting up. If Jen's dad were a horse, he'd be a Connemara—a kind, all-purpose pony that's great with kids. All the other Zuckers are lean, except for Mr. and Mrs. Zucker.

"Scoop?" Mr. Zucker asked, breathing heavy, leaning forward, his hands on his knees. "Do you think there's any hope for this horse?" He took in a long, deep breath. "Mrs. Zucker says we should sell Cheyenne and get a horse all the little Zuckers can ride."

Jen straightened her wire-rimmed glasses. "But Dad could no more sell Cheyenne than I could. He likes to look at her."

Mr. Zucker gazed back at the Paint. "As

Winston Churchill said, 'There is something about the outside of a horse that is good for the inside of a man.'" He stood up straight and stretched, holding the middle of his back the way Dotty does sometimes after bagging groceries. "Thank you for coming, Scoop."

Jen's fair skin looked pink with sunburn, and her blond hair, pinned up off her neck, looked sun-white. She wore cutoffs and a red shirt tied at her waist. She grinned at her dad in a way that made me wonder what it would be like to be a Zucker and belong in this family.

I wiped the idea out of my head. "Would you guys let me go out and try to get Cheyenne by myself?" I asked.

"Be our guest," said Travis, bowing.

Cheyenne snorted. I knew she was laughing at them. At 5 years old, she'd thrown the Zuckers off her back and into turmoil more than once.

"Cheyenne?" I called in a low voice.

She stopped, stiff-legged and tense, watching me out of the corner of her eye as I got nearer. I stopped too, still 15 feet away, and stared directly at her. That made her uneasy, and she shifted her weight and pawed the ground. I kept staring. Cheyenne snorted, then took a step in my direction.

"No," I said firmly, holding her gaze. "You can't come in here."

She stopped, confused. I spread out my arms when she craned her neck toward me. "No way," I said, as if I were preventing her approach. "Don't you come over here." A bee buzzed around my head, but I ignored it.

The mare didn't know what to do. She liked being the one in control, but she needed to belong and to be accepted. Horses aren't much different from people when it comes to that. Cheyenne glanced at me, then looked away. Finally she lowered her neck, a sign of humbling.

Cheyenne tried taking another step toward me. I held my stare and murmured, "No you don't."

She stopped and let out a little neigh. Her thick lips moved as if she were silently begging me to let her come. I lowered my gaze and turned sideways. "Okay now. Come on, Chey."

Head lowered, she walked right up to me. I scratched her jowl and withers, and she followed me over to her masters, glad to be friends again.

"Jen," I said, "why don't you give your horse some of your special homemade mash so she's glad she came?"

Jen clipped on the lead rope and rubbed Cheyenne on her white-starred forehead. "Thanks, Scoop." She turned and hollered back to her brother, "Told you, Travis. Horses have a pecking order, like wolves in a pack, and Scoop gets accepted as equal or above." She led her horse toward the barn.

I'd never thought about the pecking order of horses. But Jen reads all the time and knows all kinds of facts about horses.

"So the horses think you're a horse, Scoop?" Travis asked, grinning.

I felt my face heat up, and I couldn't look at him.

Mrs. Zucker, still toting her three babies, yelled over from the fence. "What a gift you have with horses, Scoop! King Solomon himself couldn't have done better." With the triplets in her arms and the Zucker twins tugging at her apron, she reminded me of Mother Hubbard. But as a horse, she'd be a Welsh Cob—compact, calm, and comfortable.

"Travis," said Mrs. Zucker, "why don't you give Scoop a ride home? Mind you drive careful now, Son. Scoop, tell your Aunt Dotty hey for me."

I nodded.

Standing behind Mrs. Zucker, Maggie, her horse on a lead rope, gave me the thumbs up sign. I knew she'd do anything about now to trade places with me and let Travis take *her* home. Moby snatched a can of orange soda out of Maggie's hand. Holding the can between her teeth, the horse lifted her head and guzzled.

Travis laughed out loud, a deep, musical laugh. "Truck's this way, Scoop," he said.

I hopped in the pickup with Travis. He'd only had his license about a month, so I might have been the first non-Zucker to ride with him. It felt weird to be in the truck alone together. We bounced out to the road, and I couldn't think of anything to say. I wished he'd turn on the radio to cover the silence.

Finally Travis said, "How did you get to be so good with horses, Scoop?"

I shrugged. I couldn't find the seatbelt, and I didn't know how close to sit to him. I was almost hugging the door. I hoped I didn't smell too much like a horse.

"You're like those horse whisperers who go around *gentling* horses instead of breaking them. You ought to do this for a living, you know?"

Gentling horses was what I wanted to do more than anything in the whole world. I wanted to tell that to Travis, but I knew I wouldn't get the words right. I turned to the open window and let the wind hit my face. We didn't say another word until we reached my house.

Travis stopped, and I got out. I waved and said, "Thanks, Travis," but I don't know if he heard me. I watched the pickup try to turn in the lane, slide one wheel in the ditch, back out, and hit the road.

I trotted inside, surprised the house was so dark. Dotty had been working late at the grocery store all week, but my brother should have been home watching television.

"Hey, B.C.!" I yelled. I tried to get to the light bulb and stumbled over a pile of something. I jerked the overhead string and the light clicked on, showing me I'd tripped over a pile of bottle caps.

My heart sped up. Before the accident, Dad used to come home from the bottle cap plant every night with a pocketful of metal bottle caps for my brother. B.C. had saved every single one of those caps. First he played with the hard, round, circles of metal by making a noisy sandpile, scooping up caps, and dumping them out. Later he used the bottle caps for toy soldiers and army men, lining them in battle formations.

I got a tight feeling in my chest. "B.C.!" I yelled, running through the house. I looked in his room, which used to be a laundry room before B.C. was born. On his bed were more bottle caps in piles, sorted in one of the hundreds of ways he sorts them. On his dresser was a bottle cap cat he'd made all by himself with nothing but Super Glue and his bottle caps. The cat was on its side. No trace of B.C.

In the living room, the coffee table was overturned. I looked around, panicked like a horse under gunfire. Then I saw a piece of paper on the floor. I picked it up. The handwriting looked familiar. *Dotty, my father needs to talk to you. Call him tonight. Stephen Dalton.*

Horsefeathers! "Stephen Dalton!" I said through clenched teeth. He'd been here with B.C. "What have you done to my brother?"

That's when I remembered to pray. I didn't get the words right in my head, but my heart was asking that God wouldn't let anything bad happen to B.C. I threw Stephen's note on the floor and raced outside. "B.C!" I yelled.

Dink. Clink. Something plopped on the step behind me. Bottle caps! I looked up and saw something move in the shadow of the chimney. I knew it was B.C. We both did a good deal of our thinking on roofs.

I ran to the side of the house and climbed the willow that hung over the roof. The branches swished softly against the house as I hurried from limb to limb. B.C. was leaning against the chimney, tossing bottle caps off the roof.

I fought the urge to yell at him. "Hey, B.C.," I said in as regular a voice as I could. "What's up?"

Only then did he look up. And when he did, he frowned at me as if he didn't know me. I eased myself down next to him. He held his hands up, like a surgeon keeping sterile. He had a bottle cap balanced on the tip of each finger.

"What's wrong, B.C.?" I asked.

After a couple of minutes, in a voice he might have used to say, "Today is Saturday," B.C. announced, "Now Grandpa Coop is dying too."

B.C., honey, how many times do I got to tell you? Your grandaddy ain't dying! He's just ... doing poorly. And we're going to trust God with that, ain't we, Hon?" Dotty poured grapefruit juice while B.C. and I scarfed down Tastee-O's, the cereal of the week at Hy-Klas. It was Monday, and we were running late.

"That's what Stephen must have been hinting at Saturday," I said, remembering his *horsefeathers* comment. I brushed a Tastee-O off Dotty's sleeve. "See, B.C., I told you not to believe anything that rat Stephen says."

It had taken me an hour to talk B.C. off the roof Saturday night. And it had taken Dotty another two hours to get him to sleep. B.C. had refused to leave Dotty during Sunday school the next morning. Then right in the middle of the church sermon, he stood up and asked everybody to pray for Grandfather Coop. But this morning he at least looked ready for school.

"I've got to run, Dotty," I said. "Thanks for breakfast." I hugged B.C. and whispered in his ear, "Don't worry about Stephen. I'll take care of him."

"I heard that, Sarah Coop," Dotty said, not raising her voice. I used to think she never raised her voice because Mr. Ford at the grocery store wore her out. But that's not it. She really does practice what she preaches and turns things over to God fast.

Every day Dotty wore black knit slacks with sewn pleats like leg stripes. The large, orange shirt hugged and bunched at her hips. She's short and what Maggie calls "pleasingly plump," with thin, straight brown hair and glasses that cover most of her face. But somehow, even now as she narrowed her hazel eyes at me, she managed to look angelic, like she should glow. Dotty's a quarter horse, strong, reliable, good for all ages.

"Stephen shouldn't oughta said nothing to B.C., Scoop," she said. "Ow!" She sucked the finger she'd just stuck with the pin of her plastic nametag. "But Jesus died for Stephen's sins too. That boy's got his own problems. There." She straightened the tag that read *Hi! I'm Dottie!*, spelled wrong.

I was thinking about how I'd like to give Stephen a few problems, but I kept my thoughts to myself and headed for the barn.

In five minutes I was walking into Orphan's barn. Shafts of light forced their way inside through huge cracks between boards. The white gold beams crossed just inside the doorway, like a Star Wars welcome. In the Coop barn, the wood is real barn wood, rough gray and splintered. And even when it's dry, it smells wet. Hay dust floated above me in the light as I dug in and mucked the stalls.

Orphan hung around while I picked Punch and Judy's hooves. After feeding and brushing the horses, I turned them out together with Orphan. They bucked and kicked for joy at their freedom.

I was running too late to check on Grandad Coop, even if I had worked up enough nerve to talk to him. I kicked off my barn boots, pulled on my tennis shoes, and hurried to West Salem Middle School. I'd never get there in time to settle the score with Stephen.

Everybody had already gone inside by the time I reached the school building, so I knew I was in trouble. As I stumbled up the broken sidewalk, I tried to imagine how it would look to Carla and Carl. Stubby grass poked through cracks in the cement, and there wasn't a level sidewalk square anywhere.

Dotty said this was the same building Dad and even Grandad Coop had gone to when they were kids. Then, it was all one room, where our gym is. Each time the town saved up enough money, they built something onto the school. So now it looked like somebody had played blocks and set down chunks wherever they liked. I'd never thought about how my school would look to somebody seeing it for the first time. Probably pretty shabby.

I eased into homeroom, hoping to see Carl. But what I saw stopped me cold. There—in *my* seat, behind *my* desk, right in front of Mrs. Gopher—sat Carla Buckingham! The only good thing about my homeroom had been where I sat, alphabetically between Maggie Brown and Ray Cravens.

"Hello," said Mrs. Gopher when she spotted me. "Come on in, Sally."

After almost a whole year of school, Mrs. Gopher still couldn't keep my name straight. I'd given up correcting her. In every other way, she was real smart and even kind of nice. And she had a great smile that showed every one of her white teeth. She just couldn't get a handle on my name.

"This is Carla Buckingham, a new student from Lexington, Kentucky." Mrs. Gopher said it smiling at the invader, pronouncing *her* name exactly right. Carla didn't bother to turn around.

"I know," I said, still standing like I didn't belong there.

Maggie must have arrived late too. She plopped in her chair, then shook hands with Carla. "I'm Maggie 37 Maroon," she said, in a pretty good fake Southern accent. Maggie's hair

46

was piled high on her head. She wore a short-sleeved, high-necked maroon dress. "My mother's lucky number is 37, and I was born on March 7 (Get it? 3–7?). So that's how I got my middle name—37."

Mrs. Gopher frowned at her attendance book. "*Maroon* today, Margaret?"

Maggie didn't miss a beat. "Possible stage name."

Meanwhile I was stalled in the back of the room, waiting for my seat.

"We've had to change things around a bit," Mrs. Gopher explained. "Just find an empty seat, Sally. I knew you wouldn't mind."

Right! Like she wouldn't mind if I replaced her with a new teacher, gave *her* seat away without even asking. Still, what was I supposed to say? I knew enough not to say what I was thinking.

"Scoop!" Jen Zucker called from the last seat in the last row. "Come join the alphabetically challenged." Then she went back to reading her book, *Theories of Western Horsemanship*.

I took the empty seat between Jen Zucker and Wayne Wilson, who looked asleep, face down on his desk. Now I was farther from the window, which I hated. And farther from Mrs. Gopher, which I would have liked under ordinary circumstances. But these were no ordinary circumstances.

From where I sat I could see Carla's shiny, black hair flowing over the back of my old chair. I felt for my own hair. I'd pulled it back, but sweaty strands were already breaking away. A piece of hay fell when I tried to tighten my ponytail.

Wayne woke up. "Wow!" he muttered. "Who's the fox?"

I glanced around the room. About half the guys had goofy looks on their faces—even Ray. Just my luck. We got Carla, and Carl had to go to Mrs. Russell's homeroom. I wondered if they'd be open for a trade. I'd gladly throw in Wayne Wilson and all the other googly-eyed eighth-grade boys. I couldn't wait to get out of middle school. High school had to be better than this.

The bell rang, and kids scurried to the hall. I let everybody else's energy kind of pull me along from class to class. Except for homeroom, I didn't see Carl or Carla all morning. I saw Stephen once, but the bell rang before I could get to him.

Maggie wasn't eating lunch, so I sat with Jen at an otherwise empty table. Jen was wearing denim shorts and a white button-down, cotton shirt without a single wrinkle in it.

"Jen," I said, picking at the fried, square fish on my tray, "did you have Carl in any of your classes?"

Jen raised her eyebrows at me over her copy of *Everything You Always Wanted to Know about*

Horses but Didn't Know Enough to Ask. "She was in art second period. She's pretty good."

"Not Carla," I said. "Carl. Her twin brother. Didn't Maggie tell you about him?"

Jen shrugged and went back to her book. "Listen to this: 'During WWI, a small group of young English girls ran a home for so-called untameable horses. The British army sent the girls all horses that were slated to be destroyed. The young horsewomen gentled every single horse with nothing but love and horse sense.' That sounds like you, Scoop, and your dream home for horses."

"It does, doesn't it?" I agreed. That's what I'd wanted to tell Travis about in his pickup. Why were horses so much easier to talk to than humans?

Ray slid in across the table from me, something he almost never does at school anymore. "So tell me all you know about the new girl." He was almost drooling.

I didn't want to talk about Carla. "Have you met her twin brother Carl? He's really nice, Ray."

"So there *is* a twin then?" Ray said. "I thought maybe you missed that one. Why wasn't he in the car?"

"What car?" I asked.

"The big, black car? The one Carla came to school in. Where've you been, Scoop?" He surveyed the cafeteria while he talked. "A limo dropped Carla off at school this morning. I can't believe you missed it."

"I was late," I explained, while Jen kept turning pages. "So Carla comes to school in a car the size of my bedroom, and her brother had to walk? I don't get it."

"David!" Without another word, Ray ran off to hang with some of the guys on the basketball team.

"Scoop?" Jen said without looking up. "Did you know that horses have the biggest eyes of any land animal in the world?"

"I'm going to look for Carl ... or Maggie, to see what she knows," I said, getting up.

Jen mumbled, "Uh huh."

I finally found Maggie putting on makeup in the girls' bathroom. I washed my hands, being careful not to look at myself in the mirror. I almost never go in the girls' bathroom. I never use the toilets. I'd rather burst. And I hate mirrors.

I didn't look away fast enough though. I caught a glimpse of my hair, frizzed all around my face from the heat, and my ponytail, so pitiful I tugged the rubber band out. I know my face and my shape aren't bad. I'm just not fancy like Maggie, or intelligent-looking like Jen. Dotty's biggest compliment for me on Sunday morning is that I look "clean and neat."

Maggie, on the other hand, spends every

spare school minute right in front of this smudged and cracked mirror. "I can't get my hair right," she said, brushing her long, brown curls to the side.

Maggie Brown, alias Green, alias Blue, alias Rose, alias Maroon, changes her look at least once a day. And not just hair and makeup either. She had traded in her morning Southern drawl for a French accent. "Eet iz being so difficile!" she said.

Maggie hadn't seen Carl either. The bell rang, and we were shoved along by a herd of girls leaving the bathroom. That's when I got an idea. "Maggie," I said, "Carl must be sick today! That's why nobody's seen him." Something inside me twinged and I thought of Grandad Coop—*doing poorly*, Dotty said. I pushed him back farther in my mind. Everybody gets sick. And Stephen was just trying to mess with B.C.'s head the way he'd tried with me.

I had to get to English, but I spotted Mrs. Gopher down the hall. I pushed through the sea of students to get to her. "Mrs. Gopher?" I caught her going into her science room. "Mrs. Gopher, is Carl going to be in our homeroom?" A huge eighth grader pushed right between us to get into the classroom. He smelled like the locker room.

"Yes, of course she is, Sally," she said.

"No, not *her*. Not Carla. *Carl*. Will we get

him too? Or will he go to Mrs. Russell's home-room?"

Mrs. Gopher looked down at me. I forgot to say that she's about twice as tall as I am, and pencil-skinny. "Carl? There is no Carl. It's Carla."

"I mean her twin brother. He said he was going to be in ninth grade next year. I just wondered if he's out sick today."

"I'm afraid you've gotten it mixed up, dear," she said. "We've only received registration for one new student. Carla Buckingham is an only child."

I got a C– on the English quiz and spaced out in science. *Carla Buckingham is an only child?* Mrs. Gopher's words drowned out everything else until the last bell rang.

Outside I caught up with Jen and Maggie by the bikes and told them what Mrs. Gopher said. "Why would she say there's only one Buckingham?" I asked. "Carla's definitely not an only child."

Jen strapped her books to her bike carrier. "Why indeed?" she asked, kicking up the kickstand. "A) School registrations got mixed up since West Salem Middle School isn't exactly used to twins. B) The Gophers are really teeneating monsters in disguise and they've devoured Carla's brother. Or, C) There really is no Carl and you've gone off the deep end or seen a ghost."

"Well, I'll know soon enough," I said. "Carl asked me to meet him after school. I'm going there right now. Want to come?"

The combination lock clicked, and Jen

unchained her bike. "Sorry, Scoop. I have to get home and guard the Little Zuckers." She mounted her bike and tucked her blond hair behind her ears. "I'll kiss Cheyenne for you though."

Maggie wheeled her bike out of the rack as Jen pedaled off. "I've got ballet lessons, Scoop," she said. "Besides, if Carl's sick he probably can't hang out anyway, *n'est-ce pas*? Call me! *Au revoir*!" Maggie biked down the road, two sixth-grade boys tagging after her, part of Maggie's fan club.

I caught sight of Stephen sneaking out the band room door. A candy bar stuck out from between his teeth. He was hopping on one foot, juggling his green nylon backpack.

"Stephen Dalton!" I screamed. "Hold your horses!" I ran after him, thinking about sweet, trusting B.C. taking in every slimy word Stephen said to upset him. Grandad Coop may not have been a prize as grandfathers go, but he meant something to B.C.

Before I could stop him, Stephen hopped into his mother's red BMW. He hollered out the window, "Scoop! Have you talked to the old man? He's got a surprise for you!"

I stopped. A wave of nausea raced through me, but I wouldn't let my mind try to figure it out. Grandad Coop was sick. No big deal. Certainly no big surprise. But Stephen Dalton still thought he had something on me.

Why me? Why a surprise for *me*?

He was doing it again, on purpose, making me crazy. *Stephen Dalton*. I just hoped this wasn't one of the times God was reading my heart.

Nothing's too long of a walk in West Salem. My house, Orphan's barn, and Dalton Stables lie in a big triangle, a triangle Ralph Dalton had been trying to take over for as long as I could remember. I had to walk past the Hy-Klas where Dotty works. I looked up and saw B.C. waving at me from the roof of the store. He looked like a weathervane.

"Hey, B.C.!" I hollered. He smiled. It's a safe roof with a long, flat area to sit and think. I put in a lot of thinking time there myself, even before Mr. Ford caught me shoplifting.

I was 10 when I started to steal gum—only single packets, and never the same color twice. I didn't even chew the gum. And most of the time I put it back the next day, straightening the rows of shiny packs neater than they'd been before.

That was when they'd nabbed me—straightening the packs—putting back instead of stealing, although nobody believed me.

The school psychologist told Dotty I wanted to get caught. But I don't think it really mattered to me one way or the other. My folks had been dead for three years, but for some reason it started to feel like they'd just died. That was a rough summer and not much mattered. Except when Dotty found out, I'd have given anything to take back the hurt I saw on her face.

Mr. Ford had held onto my shirt collar and called Dotty away from checkout to tell her I was shoplifting. Even then she didn't raise her voice, but I caught a flash of the pain that stabbed her behind her eyes. She just put her arm around me, took off her apron and told Mr. Ford, "Will you excuse us, please? I'm taking a break now."

Then she climbed the fire escape to the roof, the first and last time she ever went on a roof to my knowledge. "Scoop," she said once we were both sitting cross-legged on the flat part. She pulled out a little red New Testament she carries on her at all times. "You and me are going to have a serious talk about Jesus."

"Jesus?" I asked. "What about Wrigley? Or Bazooka?" I was sorry as soon as I said it because the hurt lines sank deeper into her wide forehead.

"Honey, I know you miss your folks—the ones you never met, and the ones you did. Emma and Ben Coop was good people, and I miss my sister more than you'll ever know." She paused and shut her eyes. Her throat twitched, like she was trying to swallow. Then she stared at me, hard. "But Emma and Ben didn't take you to church. And with me working most Sundays for Mr. Ford, I haven't churched you much better. I should have done so, and I apologize." (*She* apologized.)

I felt so many tears inside pushing to get out, like hot lava forcing its way through rock. I tried to swallow the salty tears.

"So I'm asking you straight out, Scoop," Dotty said, looking through my eyes to my insides. "Have you trusted Christ to forgive your sins, Honey? He died for you, Scoop. And He rose from the dead so He can make you a part of His family."

I couldn't look at her. I could barely breathe. *Part of Jesus' family?* Finally I shook my head. I didn't feel like I was part of anybody's family.

"Well," she said, "don't you think this would be as good a time as any?"

I nodded. And we prayed together right on that roof, even when it started to rain. "Lord, You know Scoop and I, we ain't the best people." Dotty said the words out loud, and I said them inside, with God hearing the words better than I could say them. "We've done some mighty bad things, and deserve Your punishment. But You've seen fit to forgive us, to give us new life with You. Give us the strength to believe in You, and the faith to know we will be in Your family in heaven." And all the while, the rain clattering on the roof sounded like angels clapping.

Dotty told Mr. Ford she couldn't work Sundays from then on. I knew I'd let Dotty and Jesus down over and over since then. But one thing—I never doubted Jesus heard our prayer on that roof. I don't think Grandad Coop ever forgave me for stealing, but I know Dotty and Jesus did.

"Hey, Scoop!" Stephen's yell brought me back to the present. He was leaning out of his mom's car at the town's only stoplight. "What's black and orange and sticky all over?" Without waiting for an answer I'd never give, he said, "Scooper Orphan Glue!"

I acted like I hadn't heard him as they drove off. But his cackle echoed in my head the whole way to Orphan's pasture. I didn't want to think about Stephen or Carla or anything else. I needed to be with Orphan.

Orphan trotted up to the gate to meet me. "Hey, Girl," I murmured, surprised as always that she's as glad to see me as I am to see her. She'd gotten herself almost completely clean, but I brushed her anyway, smoothing out my own worries as I smoothed her shiny coat.

We set out for Carl's, me riding bareback with a hackamore—not much more than a leather halter with reins. Orphan pranced and seemed on alert. All of a sudden the sky grew darker and the smell of pines and walnuts sharpened. Clouds sped across the sky as if they were in a heavenly race. Buckingham Palace loomed above the trees.

I stopped in the backyard and slid to the ground. What would I say if Carla came out? Carl probably hadn't told his sister he'd invited me over. If she found me lurking outside, Carla might even think I'd come to steal her stupid bridle or something, especially if Stephen had gotten to her. Orphan nudged me with her muzzle. I broke the carrot in my pocket and gave her half.

I had almost worked up enough courage to knock on the front door when I felt something at my shoulder. I must have jumped. Orphan lunged back so hard I let go of the reins. "Carl!"

There he stood, this time with a New York Yankees cap on backwards, but the same baggy sweatshirt.

"You okay?" I asked.

"Sure I'm okay," he answered, grinning, but not looking directly at me. He scratched behind Orphan's ears.

"But you weren't in school today."

"I told you I might not be," he said, looking up at the dark clouds. The air smelled of storm and felt charged with electricity. The hairs on my arms stood up.

"But—" I began. What was I supposed to say? That his sister acted like he didn't exist and everybody thought Carla was an only child?

None of my business. Still, I couldn't let it go. "Nobody at school knows you're going there."

"Yeah?" He frowned up at the sky while I waited for him to explain. But he didn't explain. It was clear he didn't plan to say any more about it.

I checked to make sure Carla wasn't around. I didn't want to get in the middle of a brother and sister fight. He'd find out soon enough about school. "So can you go to Dalton Stables?"

Carl glanced nervously over his shoulder, then shrugged. "To practice for the show?"

I'd forgotten all about the big West Salem Horse Show. "No. Just to visit your horse," I said.

The idea seemed like a new one to Carl. But he followed on the other side of Orphan as I headed for the stables. For some reason, I felt relieved to move away from that house.

"You know," I said, "you ought to give your horse, Buckingham's British Pride, a real name—like Buck or Ham."

Carl laughed. "You definitely don't know Mother."

We reached the cobblestone drive that leads onto the Dalton Stables grounds. People love the rounded stone entrance. Horses hate it, and Orphan stopped.

"I have an idea," Carl said. "Why don't I

stay here with Orphan and you go look in on Buckingham's Pride?"

That made me mad. I was so sick of people looking down on Orphan just because she didn't have papers. "Why? Isn't Orphan good enough for *Ham*? Don't want to mix the stable royalty with backyard horses? Well Orphan is a hundred times better—"

"Backyard horses?" Carl asked, his eyes narrowing.

"Yeah, backyard horses. You know, the kind of horse that grows up with a kid in her backyard—like Orphan and me, or Moby and Maggie, or Cheyenne and Jen. We don't stable them. We don't show them."

"You mean you don't show in horse shows?" Carl asked.

"No. Is it so hard to believe that we have horses as friends instead of jumpers or show horses?"

"Look, it's not what you think. I—it's just that I didn't tell the stables I might come by today. They're not expecting me."

"You mean you have to make an appointment to see your own horse? Horsefeathers! When I have *my* stables, every horse will be a backyard horse. No appointments allowed."

Carl took Orphan's lead from me. "Just go in first. If nobody's there, holler and I'll bring Orphan in."

I shrugged and went ahead. Ham whinnied as I entered the barn. Dalton Stables has the feel of a hotel. A crew of stable hands keeps everything clean and orderly. It smelled more like lemon cleaner than horse.

Stephen's horse Champion pawed the ground in the first stall. He wore a red stable blanket, a fly mask, and leg wraps. When I got close, he flattened his ears as if he'd love to take a bite out of me. As I passed him, I murmured, "Champion, are you being a good host?" One ear flicked up, then flattened back down. He stretched out his neck, ready to attack. Ribbons, trophies, and pictures of Stephen and his sorrel framed the stall. He'd been the champion in our show circuit for two years straight.

It was growing dark, and probably everyone had gone home for dinner. I clicked on the light and hollered for Carl.

Orphan got skittish as Carl led her down the walkway. "Scoop?" he called. "You sure nobody's here?"

I still didn't get why we were sneaking in. Orphan stopped in front of Ham's stall and snorted.

"Buckingham's British Pride, I'd like you to meet Orphan," Carl said.

"Orphan," I said, joining them and taking the reins from Carl, "this is Ham." Orphan's nostrils grew big, and the two horses sniffed, touched muzzles, and cleared their throats at each other. Then they blew into one another's nostrils.

"They're beautiful together, aren't they?" Carl said.

"Ham's mane and tail shine like silk," I said. Both tail and mane stuck out from under a navy blue stable blanket.

A door slammed at the far end of the barn. I turned to look. Stephen Dalton walked in and hung up a bridle. Then he seemed to spot me.

"You gotta meet—" I turned for Carl, but he wasn't there.

"Still talking to horses, Scoop?" Stephen asked, coming my way. "Are they answering yet?"

I moved around Orphan to look down the other line of stalls. Carl had disappeared. Evaporated, as if he'd never been there at all.

7

The only non-horses in Dalton Stables were Stephen Dalton and me. "I thought I smelled a nag that didn't belong here," he said, looking down his upturned nose at Orphan.

For once Stephen was right. Orphan didn't belong here, and neither did I. I turned to leave, then remembered B.C. "You've got your nerve, Stephen Dalton! Just stay away from B.C. If you *ever* upset him like that again—"

"Yeah, yeah. Listen, Scoop. I don't know what you're doing here," Stephen said, as if he hadn't even heard me. "But I'm glad I found you."

I glared at him, a sick feeling crawling into my veins. Of all things he might have said, that one worried me the most. Stephen Dalton was never glad to see me. "Why?" I asked, my voice cracking.

"I guess you still haven't talked to Grandad Coop or you'd know why," Stephen answered. "The old man has finally given up—cashed in his chips. He's moving into the nursing home.

Dad's buying him out. We'll probably knock that old barn of his down and—"

My ears buzzed so loud I couldn't hear anymore. "You're lying, Stephen! Grandad Coop would never sell that land!"

"He doesn't have much choice. He's not exactly all there, Scoop. Kind of flown the *coop*, if you get my drift. When's the last time you talked to the old guy?" Stephen made little circles with his index finger beside his head—crazy.

My head was swirling. I couldn't think straight. Grandad Coop couldn't sell the farm. The barn. I wouldn't let him. Without another word to Stephen, I swung up on Orphan and got out of Dalton Stables as fast as I could.

Thunder rumbled and dark clouds raced with Orphan and me to Grandad Coop's. I hugged Orphan's neck, crying into her black mane. "I won't let it happen. He won't sell your barn," I whispered over and over.

At the pasture gate, I slid off Orphan and turned her loose inside. My sides were heaving, as if I'd been the one running instead of Orphan. Then I did run—all the way to Grandad's front porch. Huge drops of water splattered my arms.

I banged on the screen door's splintered wooden frame. "Grandad Coop!" I yelled. "Come out!"

No answer. I pounded so hard the door shook. "I know you're in there!" I cupped my hands around my eyes and leaned into the screen, peering into the dark kitchen.

Thunder cracked and seemed to shake the porch under my feet. "You can't sell! Do you hear me?" I screamed through the screen and imagined my cries dissected into little squares, sifted through the metal mesh.

Finally his dark figure shuffled to the door. He studied me as if he didn't know who or what I could be. From where I stood on the other side of the screen, his face looked like a puzzle of a million pieces—all of them wrinkled and lined in silver. It shocked me to see how much older he looked than when I'd seen him not two months earlier.

"Stephen said you're selling out! Moving! Tell me he's making it up! Tell me!" But the pressure in my chest, like a saddle girth cinched too tight, told me I wasn't going to hear what I wanted.

The old man rubbed the back of his neck and blinked past me at the storm, as if he were searching the skies for the answer. From somewhere inside the kitchen came a putrid smell like something dying.

"I can't help it," he said, his voice flat. "Things don't stay in my head anymore." He pulled at the few tufts of white left on his head, as if he could tug thoughts out one at a time. "I'm so tired." He shook his head, then turned his back on me.

My whole body trembled. I pressed my face to the door and felt the cool metal dent my nose and forehead as the screen bubbled inward like metal bubble gum.

He was standing a few feet inside, thin and slumped shouldered. "Ralph's coming to fetch me for the nursing home," he muttered, his voice high like a little girl's.

The darkness inside his house swallowed him up. I rattled the door, then stuck one foot inside.

He wheeled around and charged toward me. "Go on, git!" His fierce cry froze me half inside, half out. "What are you doing around here? If you're stealing from me, I'll call the po-lice, you hear?"

His words stung. Burning tears swelled my head, pressing their way out. I spun around on the porch. Orphan's whinny pierced the thunder. The screen slapped behind me as I ran through pouring rain to the barn. Orphan. That's all I wanted—to see my horse.

I stayed in the barn with Orphan until I cried myself out. She nuzzled my face and tried to get me to play with her. Finally she gave up and settled next to me.

~~~~~~~~~~~~~~~~~~~~~~~~~~~~~~

When I finally got home, Dotty was waiting for me. "Scoop! Ain't you got enough

67

sense to come in out of the rain? You're soaked clean through and shivering like a humming-bird!"

B.C. was already in bed. Something had happened to upset him in school. He'd come home and hidden under his covers until he fell asleep.

While Dotty ran the bath water and got me a flannel nightgown, I told her everything. About Stephen. About Grandad Coop. About Ralph Dalton planning to take over. But I couldn't bring myself to ask what was deepest in my heart. What would happen to Orphan?

When I got to the part about Ralph signing Grandad up for the nursing home, Dotty bit her lip and set bottles and soap down harder than she needed to. But the only thing she said was, "We need to pray about this. God will know what to do."

The rain had stopped when I got out of the tub. I lay in my attic room and stared out at stars that poked through the clouds. My bed sits under the window, and the ceiling slants down on both sides like the letter A.

Starlight illuminated my room in a pale, streaked glow—my horse posters, the horse statues on my dresser, the closet I had to duck to enter.

As I did every night, I imagined folding up the world. I started with the black sky filled with the moon and stars. My window sucked them in. The stars untwinkled and folded inward. Next, the ceiling, my wall posters, and dresser were pulled into the folding vacuum. The empty bed, my closet, the window itself, my bed, my arms and legs, and me, all folded up into a void, a feeling of complete nothingness.

Every other night I'd keep imagining and let the world unfold, giving it back to God a piece at a time, releasing me, then my bed, my closet and dresser and window, the stars returning to the sky. But tonight was different. The world wouldn't unfold. I couldn't get it to unfold.

8

My whole entire world was collapsing around me, but Dotty made me go to school. From the far end of the sidewalk, I spotted Jen and Maggie hanging just outside the main doors. Jen was wiping her lenses with a man's white handkerchief. She stuck her glasses back on and stared at me. "You look awful," she said.

I told them why, leaving out the part where Grandad Coop accused me of stealing.

"Scoop," Jen said, "I am so sorry. I don't know why he's always so mean to you."

"What are you going to do?" Maggie asked, talking with her hands as much as her voice. She was dressed completely in blue with dozens of braids in her hair, each one tied with a pale blue ribbon.

"I have to buy Orphan," I said. "But even then if Grandad Coop sells the barn, I still won't have any place to keep her."

"He should let *you* run the barn. You're better with horses than he is!" Maggie insisted.

"She's better with horses than anybody is," Jen said.

I tried to smile at them. "Where would I get the money to run Grandad's horse business? Even he couldn't keep it going."

We were quiet for a minute. Then Maggie said, "I wish I could tell you to keep Orphan with us." I admit I'd been hoping she'd offer as a back-up. "But Mother plans to move us to town, even if she doesn't marry Mr. Chesley."

Maggie's mother had had so many plans, and so many husbands, I'd lost track. Her latest beau was Mr. Chesley, our science teacher. He lived in a tiny house close to school. "What about your horse if you move to town?" I asked. "What will you do with Moby?"

"I was sort of hoping to use your grandpa's place," Maggie said. "Oh, Scoop! What are we going to do?" Her eyes misted over and real tears trickled down both cheeks.

"*My* horse has been causing so much trouble, there's no way my mom would let us keep another one. Last night Cheyenne kicked the gate to pieces." Jen put one arm on each of our shoulders. "There has to be a way to keep Stephen's dad from getting your grandad's barn."

"Scoop," Maggie said, blowing her nose into a flowered handkerchief that made me think of little old ladies, "wouldn't this be the perfect time for your backyard horse stable? We could keep our horses together and—"

Stephen came strutting up, his red hair reflecting the morning's sunlight like aluminum foil. He was the only guy who hadn't come to school in jeans or shorts. "So did you talk to Grandfather Coop?" he asked. "Was I right or was I right? He's lost it. Mom told me last night it's Alzheimer's disease."

Maggie gasped and glanced at me. "Isn't that when you lose your memory?"

Stephen shrugged, but Jen explained, "Alzheimer's is a progressive disease. Brain cells break down and cause loss of memory."

I felt sick inside. All these years I hadn't wanted to get to know my grandfather. He scared me. Now I probably wouldn't get the chance. I pictured him the way Dotty had described him, handing me the bottle to feed Orphan as a foal.

"Hey!" Ray walked up before I could ask anything more about Grandad or Alzheimer's. "How's it going, guys?" Suddenly Ray's brown eyes got bigger than I'd ever seen them. I followed his gaze to the limo that had just pulled up.

Carla Buckingham stepped out in a white sundress, white sandals, and a white ribbon around her shiny, black hair. I hated to admit it, but I could see why she'd taken Ray's breath away. He'd sure never looked at me like that. She didn't seem to be part of the same world as Alzheimer's and horse problems.

Carl wasn't with her, and I guess I'd quit expecting him to be. Carla looked straight ahead, as if she didn't even realize boys were drooling over her. Ray jostled us aside to get in front of her. "Good morning, Carla," he said, looking goofy.

"Good morning," she said, sounding exactly like Carl would have, leaving off the *d* in good and the *r* and *-ing* in morning: *Goo moan*. It sounded a little like one of Maggie's accents.

Stephen laughed out loud. "Goo moan?" he repeated. "Did she just say *Goo moan*?"

Five or six kids walked past us and laughed too—at Stephen or at Carla. I didn't laugh, not out loud. But inside I was glad to have everybody see Perfect Carla in a not-so-perfect light. I asked God to forgive me for enjoying it.

The bell rang and we headed for homeroom. Mrs. Gopher was smiling at Carla and talking like they were best friends. I wondered what it would be like to be rich, to have teachers try to be your friend. It just wasn't fair. Carl was rich too, and Mrs. Gopher didn't even know he was alive.

I couldn't do anything about Grandad's problem, but I *could* do something about Carl's. Announcements were almost over. Mrs. Gopher was writing on the board. If I didn't act fast, I'd miss my chance. One way or the other I had to get the truth out of Carla Buckingham. I was going to make her tell the whole class about her twin brother.

The old pencil sharpener trick. I'd seen Stephen use it a million times. I took a deep breath and pressed hard on my pencil. The pencil wasn't very sharp to begin with, so I could barely get it to break off. It didn't make much of a sound, but I'd have a broken pencil to show if I needed it.

"Horsefeathers," I muttered, holding the pencil up for view. Jen gave me a weird look.

I began making my way over to the pencil sharpener, but with one slight detour. I side-stepped in front of two desks to end up right next to Carla Buckingham. Without coming to a full stop, I whispered, "Carla, where's Carl?"

No answer.

I took a couple of quick steps backwards and whispered again. "Where is your brother?"

She didn't even look up from her pink, flowered notebook. It made me so mad I could have flung her stupid notebook right out the window.

"Carla, where is Carl?" I guess it came out louder than I meant it to.

Mrs. Gopher turned from the board. "Sarah Coop!"

Now she remembers my name, I thought. I stood motionless, waiting for the chalk dust to fly.

Mrs. Gopher moved in front of my old desk

so I was staring up at her. Her nostrils looked huge, and her lips had disappeared altogether, as if her teeth had gobbled them up. "Since you've already disturbed the whole class, perhaps you'd like to fill us all in on what you've been whispering here."

I looked down at Carla, who pretended to study the cracks in my old desk. How could she just sit there and act like she didn't know what this was about?

"Sarah?" Mrs. Gopher wasn't about to let it go.

"I-I ... " I caught glimpses of wide-opened eyes around the room—Ray's, Jen's, Maggie's, even Wayne's, and he slept through anything. Well *I* had nothing to hide. Carla was the one everybody should have been staring at. "I just asked Carla where her brother Carl is," I blurted out.

"I don't understand," Mrs. Gopher said in that teacher-voice that lets you know they're fed up with you. "Didn't I tell you we only have one new student? What did you really say to her?"

"That was it! Honest!" I didn't know what else she thought I'd say. "But Carla wouldn't give me an answer."

"For which we are eternally grateful, Carla," Mrs. Gopher said.

But I didn't want to miss the chance for a public confession from Carla. "Would you let her tell us where her brother is?" I pressed. "Please?" I looked from Mrs. Gopher to Carla and back again.

Finally Mrs. Gopher said, "Carla, would you please do us all a favor and answer Sarah's question once and for all?"

The bell rang and footsteps thundered in the hall, but nobody in our room budged. I felt my heart pounding, like cantering horses' hooves. At least now I was going to get a straight answer.

"I don' know what 'say, Ms. Gopher," Carla said softly.

See! I wanted to scream, hearing the way she dropped letters and words. *She even talks like her brother.*

Carla, her big, brown eyes wide with innocence, looked past me to Mrs. Gopher. "The truth is, I don't have a brother."

9

"Carla's lying her socks off!" I told Jen and Maggie. It was last period, and the boys' and girls' gym classes had to run laps on the cinder track behind the school. Untrimmed lilac bushes grew in the field north of the track, and the air smelled like a mixture of lilacs and boy sweat.

"Why would Carla lie, Scoop?" Maggie asked, stepping higher than she needed to as we jogged lap one.

"I can think of a lot of reasons," I said. "And none of them any good. Maybe she hates Carl." I imagined Carl, his baseball cap off to one side, tied up and gagged inside a Mayflower moving van on its way back to Kentucky.

"Give it a rest, Scoop," Jen said. She was walking on the other side of Maggie, but going the same speed as our jogging. Coach Lee blew his whistle at us to speed up. I jogged faster. Maggie stepped higher. Jen took bigger walking strides. "There must be a reasonable explanation," Jen insisted.

Stephen Dalton kept to the far side of the track, away from us, until the cool-off lap. When Maggie and Jen ran in to change, Stephen walked up beside me, his face redder than usual. His eyes darted around in grayish-green pools, like pond scum. I could tell he had something he was dying to tell me, so I waited, focusing on a pimple on his upper lip.

"We sold her!" he exclaimed.

I stopped breathing. I opened my mouth, but the words choked each other off.

"No lie," he said. "My dad sold Orphan—in an auction." He tried to wipe the smirk off his face. "I'm really sorry I had to be the one to tell you, Sarah."

Stephen's pimple grew blurry. And then I couldn't see his face at all. Everything blurred together as tears bubbled over and leaked out.

I ran off the track and out of the school yard as the last bell rang. I didn't slow until I was out of town. I crossed a freshly plowed field that seemed like an ocean of tiny, black waves. Twice I stumbled and could hear my own heavy breathing as if it belonged to someone else far away.

I raced under the buzzard tree, scaring up dozens of complaining birds who exploded upward in a flurry of black wings and angry caws.

I reached the old Coop barn, stopped, and leaned against the rough wood to catch my breath before I went in. Stephen Dalton was nothing but a liar, I told myself. I'd find Orphan in her stall, the same stall where she was born, the same stall where I'd spent the night under a horse blanket with my mom.

I slid open the barn door. It groaned, then thudded in place. The familiar barn smell of straw and manure gave me confidence that nothing had changed. Everything would be just like it always had been.

Except I didn't hear Orphan's nicker. I listened, but I didn't hear it.

I turned the corner, stood before Orphan's stall, and pushed the stall door. Orphan was gone. The stall was empty.

That didn't mean anything. Why shouldn't Orphan's stall be empty? Orphan loves the outdoors too much to stay in her stall all day. She'd be in the pasture, grazing, waiting for me.

I raced out to the paddock. "Orphan!" I yelled. "Orphan!" But nobody came.

I stood on the fence and hollered into the pasture for her. The wind picked up and blew my hair across my face. Maple wings twirled through the air like tiny, angry dancers. "Orphan!" I screamed. Her name blew back at me as if the wind rejected it.

There was no horse in sight.

I ran back inside the barn and into Orphan's stall. I grabbed the feed trough and flung it against the wall. I kicked the stall and banged on the walls until my hands bled. Finally, I slid to the ground, wrapped my arms around my knees, and sobbed.

I don't have any idea how long I sat like that before I heard the stall door creak. I looked up to see Carl.

"Scoop?" he said softly. "Is it true? Did Stephen's dad really sell Orphan? Did he?"

I felt a lump blocking my throat, and I wished he would go away. "Leave me alone," I said, my voice hoarse and raspy.

Carl knelt down and put a hand on my arm. His hand was surprisingly soft and small, like a girl's. "We'll fix it," he said, in his stupid, mushy voice. "We have to. Maybe it's not too late. Get your aunt to talk to Stephen's father. Maybe she could buy Orphan back."

I shook his hand off my arm. "Horsefeathers, Carl! Don't you get it?" I felt the volcano that had been building up inside me erupt in a fury. I laughed one, harsh *ha* that didn't sound like me or anyone I knew. "Dotty buy Orphan?"

"*Someone* in your family has to help," he said.

"My family? Someone in my *family*? I don't have a family!" I screamed. "Not like you. There's nobody to help!" I was shaking, breathing harder than when I'd run all that way. "All I had was Orphan, Carl. And now I don't have her." I hid my head so Carl wouldn't see me cry. I'd never felt so alone. Even my heart had stopped praying.

Thunder rumbled in the distance.

"Wait here," Carl said.

When I looked up, he was gone too. I was in the stall alone. Maybe I'd been alone all the time. Maybe Carl *wasn't* real. I didn't care. Orphan was real. Orphan was gone.

I'm not sure how much time had passed when I heard a ping, plunking on the metal roof of the barn. It was starting to rain—hard. The clatter grew louder, a metallic banging as if a thousand prisoners were beating their knives on tin plates demanding more.

I squeezed my eyes shut and covered my ears. As the rain came down harder and harder, I felt like I was in the middle of a giant flood, and I was the only one who'd made it onto the ark before the door slammed shut and trapped the world on the other side.

The stall door flung open and in came water-soaked Carl. He sat cross-legged in front of me, water dripping from his baseball cap, a Padres cap. A mini stream flowed from his brim to his nose and down to the straw. Carl stared into my eyes, and for the first time didn't look away.

"Horsefeathers," he said. When Carl said it, it sounded like *horfedder*, and I almost grinned.

Then he held up a long, grayish-brown feather, tipped with white.

I took the feather from him and ran my hand down the soft, wet bristles. "You telling me this is a horsefeather?" I asked.

"It's a cuckoo feather," Carl explained. "My father brought it back from the Tropics a long time ago."

I looked at Carl's soaking wet sweatshirt and jeans. "You ran all the way in the pouring rain to get a cuckoo feather?" I asked.

He nodded. "I want you to have it."

"A cuckoo feather? Are you trying to tell me something here, Carl? I mean, I get the picture. Everybody at school thinks I'm cuckoo."

But Carl looked dead serious. "Cuckoo birds are hard to understand. For some reason, they have to give up their young. Nobody knows why they do it."

I felt more warm tears trying to break loose, but I fought them back. Nobody had ever told me why I was given up for adoption. And I'd never asked.

Carl moved in closer. "After the mother cuckoo lays her egg, she knows she can't sit on it herself. Maybe she can't sit still that long, or maybe she knows she'd make a poor mother. So she carries that egg ever so carefully and flies around and around with it—no matter how long it takes her—until she finds the perfect nest for her baby cuckoo."

I remembered something Dotty had said while we were on the Hy-Klas roof after I got caught shoplifting. She'd said we should be thankful for the woman I was born to, the woman who had me. That woman had cared enough to find exactly the right parents for me. And God had been in charge of the whole thing.

Carl went on, his words sounding clearer to me, not hard to make out. "The mother cuckoo puts her egg in the perfect nest and flies off. When the egg hatches, the baby is raised by the new parent bird, just as if it had always belonged in her family."

"Horsefeathers," I said, turning the feather in my hand, studying its little, bone-like parts. The stem curved, with each tiny offshoot fitting neatly into the main branch.

The barn flashed with light, thunder broke, and a new burst of rain hit the roof. I tried to thank Carl, but the rain bashed the barn. Carl couldn't have heard me no matter how loud I shouted.

We sat in loud silence for a long time, me twirling the feather, Carl chewing on a piece of straw. I didn't even notice when the rain let up.

Finally, Carl got to his feet, shook his legs out, and sloshed over to the window. He wiped the foggy pane with the sleeve of his sweatshirt. "Scoop!" he shouted. "Come here! Quick!"

"What is it?" I asked, thinking it might be a rainbow. I walked over to the window and peered out. The sun breaking behind the field outlined the shape of a horse and somebody with it.

"It's not ... ?" Carl began.

"Orphan," I whispered. I tucked my horse-feather into my jeans and tore out of the barn. "Orphan!" I screamed.

Orphan whinnied back, then did it again, high and shrill. Ralph Dalton had her on a lead rope, and Stephen walked behind his dad. She jerked loose and galloped toward me.

I ran to meet my horse. The pasture had turned to mud, and my feet slipped. I caught my balance and kept running toward her as she raced toward me. Orphan stopped short in front of me, and I threw my arms around her neck. I breathed her, burying my face in her wet mane. "Orphan, you came back," I murmured, my tears getting lost in rain and sweat.

Ralph Dalton, in high mud boots, trod carefully across the sloppy pasture. When he reached us, he pulled off leather riding gloves and slapped them lightly against his leg. "Sarah," he said, as if he were glad to see me.

"Stephen said you sold Orphan!" I shouted, shooting Stephen a look to kill.

"That's what he said," Stephen shot back. He stood behind his father, as if using him for a shield.

"I took the 2-year-olds to the Hamilton auction and got a good price for them," said Stephen's dad. "Orphan went along just to see what she'd bring without papers. She didn't price out well."

I still had my arms locked around Orphan's neck. I wanted to drown myself in her wet horse smell. The rain on her neck felt cold against my cheek.

"You're fond of this horse, aren't you, Sarah?" asked Ralph Dalton. "You should see if Dotty can come up with some cash. Anyway, one way or the other, we'll just have 'til the end of the month to find a home for Orphan." He eyed the barn. "That's when the bank note comes due. They'll foreclose if Dad Coop can't make the payment again."

"Foreclose on the farm?" I repeated, imagining heroines on railroad tracks and villains with mustaches. It all seemed too unreal, like a play ... or a nightmare.

"Don't worry," he said. "We'd never let that happen. I'm quite willing to buy out Dad Coop and save the land. I know it's been in my wife's family for years. It would be a shame to see the property pass out of the family."

I felt like this was all happening to someone else. I hadn't finished being grateful that Orphan was back. She hadn't been sold. I was holding her right now. I should have been thanking God.

But a deeper panic swept over me, making me so light-headed I thought I might faint.

I swung myself up on Orphan's wet back. "Come on, Girl," I whispered. "Let's get out of here!" Orphan answered me with a surge of power, rearing off the ground and lunging into the muddy pasture.

I heard Stephen and his dad hollering, but Orphan and I kept going, galloping toward the barn, leaving them stranded in the field. Orphan slowed to a trot at the paddock gate. I'd left it open, and she pranced through to the paddock and up to the barn door.

"Carl!" I yelled into the barn.

No answer.

I leaned down, hugged Orphan's neck so I wouldn't bump my head, and urged her into the barn. "Carl!" I called. "Where are you?" My voice echoed down the empty stalls.

There was no answer. Carl was gone.

I stayed in the barn another hour, brushing Orphan dry—making the hairs stand up backwards, then brushing them smooth. I thought Carl would come back. I wanted to grab a horse blanket and stay the night in Orphan's stall, but I wasn't 3 anymore.

I half-expected Stephen and his dad to storm the barn, but they must have thought better of it. Nobody came. And I knew I had to get home to Dotty and B.C.

Twice I crossed the barnyard and got out to the road, only to run back to the barn and make sure Orphan was still there. Both times she whinnied to me and acted as glad to see me as if we'd been apart for weeks.

By the time I tramped home in the mud, it was pitch dark. From the edge of our yard, I could see through the front window. The yellowed shade was pulled down halfway, but I could make out Dotty's potato-shaped outline shuffling through the arched, open doorway between the kitchen and living room.

The room looked golden through the shade, like a different world from the one Orphan and I were stuck in. How was I going to get Dotty to help me buy Orphan before Stephen and his dad really did sell her?

I walked around to the kitchen door and heard voices. I stopped, my hand on the door-knob.

"*Horsefeathers!*" muttered a harsh, gravelly voice.

Immediately I thought of Stephen's mocking imitation of Grandad. If Stephen Dalton had come over to upset B.C. again, I was going to make him pay! I pushed the screen open and let it slam behind me. "Stephen—!"

But instead of Stephen, there stood Grandad Coop himself, in his baggy gray slacks and white buttoned-down vest. He looked frail, but normal. "Good," he said, pointing to the table. "Your aunt made us wait supper."

"Scoop?" Dotty's holler always had some of her breath in it, as if she'd run a marathon. "Come help B.C. with the table."

My mind was still stunned, but my body moved to the kitchen table where B.C. was setting a fourth napkin. Four places, not three. "Is he eating with us?" I asked. Even on Christmas and Fourth of July, when Dotty invited all the relative-less people in town, Grandad Coop never showed.

"Yes, isn't that wonderful?" Dotty said, probably not wanting *my* answer. She stared into the open refrigerator as if she couldn't remember what she wanted.

B.C. was bouncing on his toes. "He's sleeping in my room!" he said. "I'm sleeping in yours."

"Now B.C.," Dotty said, "I told you for tonight you could bunk with me in my room." She plunked down two white Styrofoam tubs and a white paper package.

"Wait a minute!" I said. "What's he doing here? Why is he sleeping in B.C.'s room?"

"Keep your voice down, Scoop," Dotty whispered, removing the plastic lids. "Macaroni salad and salami from the counter, and some three-bean from yesterday. I couldn't let him go to a nursing home, could I?"

"Are you saying he's going to ... to live here?" Things were caving in on me so fast, I couldn't think straight. "That's not fair! It's my home too! You should have asked me!"

"I ain't saying that," Dotty whispered. "We'll just take it a step at a time and trust God to show us. Get them rolls out of that there brown bag, will you, Scoop?"

I wasn't at all hungry. My stomach still churned from the threat hanging over Orphan's head. I wanted to get Dotty by herself, to ask her about buying Orphan. And now this!

I set down the rolls hard enough to shake the table. Making as much noise as possible, I set out a pitcher of water, the pickle jar, and plastic squeeze mustard.

We took our seats around the green-and-white checked, plastic tablecloth, B.C. sitting on the kitchen stool. Dotty said grace, adding in about how thankful we all were that Grandad Coop could share a meal with us.

I peeked during her prayer. Grandad Coop didn't look any more thankful than I felt.

Dotty reached across the table and spooned a glob of macaroni on Grandad's plate and B.C's, then on hers. "Mr. Ford came by the store today," she said in the singsong voice she uses to fill silences.

Mr. Ford got quoted a lot in our house. Even though Dotty had worked for him for almost seven years, she seemed to think he might walk in any day and fire her for not looking busy enough.

"Lou was on break," she went on. "So Mr. Ford comes up to me and says, 'Dotty, we're not turning enough profit,' like it was my fault. 'Dotty, we need younger products.' 'Yes, Mr. Ford,' I says, but I ain't got the slightest notion what younger products is. So he goes on about this and that, how young people got all this money. I liked to die before Lou got back! Pass the ketchup."

My stomach twisted listening to the small talk, to Grandad Coop suck spit through his teeth after every bite, to B.C. sloshing water in his mouth and kicking the leg of his stool.

Dotty kept up the cheery chatter, but her voice drifted farther and farther away. The clock behind me ticked louder. Through the screen, the crickets chirped, harsh and steady. I stared at my plate, feeling like some inside-out hurricane, with the calm part on the outside and the raging, whirling part on the inside.

"You're not eating a bite, Scoop." Dotty sounded as disappointed as if she'd stayed up all night cooking dinner. "Does the macaroni taste old?" She lifted the Styrofoam container, brought it up to her nose and sniffed.

I gripped the sides of my chair. "Dotty, I need to buy Orphan."

Her instant silence was like shutting off water. "Oh, Scoop." She reached across and slapped two more slices of greasy salami on her plate. "Could we talk about it later?" She cocked her head sideways at Grandad.

"No!" I said, ignoring Grandad. "I'll pay you back. I promise. I'll get a job after school. And I can work all summer. You know—"

"Who took my roll?" Grandad's feeble voice still overpowered mine. We turned toward him. He had one hand in his lap. With the other hand he moved his silverware, lifted his plate, shoved

B.C.'s water glass, spilling it.

"Do you have it?" he shouted at B.C. "I won't stand for this!" He glared at Dotty. "Don't think I don't know what's going on here!"

Dotty put a hand on B.C.'s trembling shoulder, but she smiled at Grandad. "Jared, we've got plenty of rolls. Could I get you a fresh one?"

Grandad kept one hand firmly in his lap. I leaned back and saw that he had his roll there, wrapped in a napkin. "There's your—" I started.

Dotty narrowed her eyes and shook her head at me. "Scoop, will you get Grandad another roll please?"

"But—" I closed my mouth and got another roll out of the plastic bag on the kitchen counter. Then I dropped it on Grandad's plate. From behind the old man, I made a face at B.C. and pointed to Grandad's lap.

We ate in silence for a few minutes. Then I tried again. "I need the money to buy Orphan because Ralph Dalton almost sold her today. He auctioned off Punch and Judy."

"Scoop!" Dotty said, her pain showing in her eyes. "How awful, Hon! I wish there was something I could do. If I had that kind of money, I'd give it to you in a flash, Sweetheart. But I ain't got it. And even if I did ... " She glanced at Grandad, who seemed to be listening. "Where could we keep her?" She added quickly,

"But like I said, I'm flat broke. I reckon it will be all I can handle to meet the rent check on this place next month."

I turned to Grandad. He looked perfectly normal, like someone who was listening, interested. I took a shot. "Grandad," I said, "what if I helped you more with the barn? You could board horses like they do at Dalton Stables. Only we'd let them run in the pastures. We wouldn't keep them all cooped up. I could gentle them myself. I can do it if—"

He scooted his chair back and stood up. Without a word, he turned his back on me and shuffled away, his stolen dinner roll clutched in his hand.

Dotty sighed and put her head in her hands. "Poor old man," she said. "Lord, look after him." Her chair groaned as she pushed away from the table and got up. "Chocolate pudding for dessert, B.C."

Her pantlegs were bunched up and I noticed her ankles, blue lines running over them like road maps trapped under nylon. She returned to the table, carrying two plastic containers of pudding, Hy-Klas special of the week. She'd forgotten to take off her store nametag: *Hi! I'm Dottie!* I wanted to make Mr. Ford fix the tag, spell her name right. He had no right anyway to let everybody call my aunt by her first name. I forced a spoonful of pudding past the lump in my throat.

"Seventy-nine a box," she said. "I wonder if this ain't what Mr. Ford means by a younger product."

We didn't try to talk anymore. I knew I'd have to look somewhere else for help. "Thanks for dinner, Dotty," I said, getting up from the table. I reached around her chair and gave her a quick hug, feeling the *Hi! I'm Dottie!* nametag cut into my chest.

~~~~~~~~~~~~~~~~~~~~~~~~~~~~

That night in bed I closed my eyes and imagined folding up the world again. Carl's horsefeather stuck out of the small, plastic vase on my dresser, and I folded it in first. The last thing folded in was Grandad Coop, looking like he did when I was little, like a cowboy out of the Old West.

I started praying and turning things back to God, but Grandad blocked everything else. I felt if I could just get him out of the opening, everything else would unfold too.

Something crashed downstairs. My first thought was B.C. I leaped out of bed and ran barefoot down the cold stairs. I peeked into Dotty's room. She was snoring, and B.C. was sound asleep next to her. My heart felt like something warm had been poured over it—they looked so peaceful.

Shuffling noises came from B.C.'s room. I tiptoed across the kitchen and saw a line of light under the door. "Grandad?" I whispered. "Are you okay?"

The door was slightly open. I pushed it and walked in. He had on a gray robe that touched the floor. What was left of his hair stuck out, reminding me of a duck. He was bent over the bed, lifting the pillow, patting the mattress, as if trying to find something.

"Grandad?" I said, my voice cracking. "Can I get you something?"

He paced the narrow floor, his hands stroking the sides of his legs. He lifted B.C.'s bottle cap cat statue and looked under it. Then he wheeled around and picked up the pillow again.

"Grandad?" I said, taking another step inside the room. The air was thick and warm, so heavy I had to take a deep breath.

He turned and seemed to look through me, his eyes swimming in their own fog. "Where in tarnation is Reba?" he asked.

I didn't understand.

"Where's Reba?" he screamed. "She's coming for me any minute, and I can't find my blamed keys."

Reba. That had been his wife's name. Reba Coop. But she died of cancer before I was adopted. He couldn't mean her.

"Do you want me to get Dotty?" I asked.

"What are you doing here?" He glared at me, making me wish I'd stayed in bed. "Who are you? What do you want?"

"It's me, Grandad. It's Scoop. You know me. Benjamin's daughter." Those words together—Benjamin's daughter—made my eyes water and my throat burn.

"I want my keys," he pleaded.

I was afraid he was going to cry. I swallowed hard. "I'll help you find them." I got down on my hands and knees and crawled along the floor looking for keys that weren't there.

"Reba?" he said. Then he whispered to me as if it were a secret, "My wife will be here any minute."

For some reason, I wanted him to know me. It shouldn't have mattered. When he did know me, I might as well have lived on some other planet. But it mattered now. "Look at me!" I said, standing up in front of him. "It's me," I said, moving closer to him. "Scoop. Don't you remember? Scoop and Orphan?"

He backed away from me, as if he'd been hit, and sat down on the bed. For a minute, I thought I could see a spark return to his misty eyes. But he just reached behind him, grabbed the pillow and began patting the bed again.

I couldn't stand it. Suddenly it felt as if everything depended on this old man in front of me, and he didn't even know me. "Listen to me, please!" I said, while he felt under the covers. "Stephen and his dad, your son-in-law Ralph— they're going to sell Orphan and your farm. Please stop them. You're the only—"

"Ralph?" he said, turning to face me.

"Yes!" He'd heard me. He knew what I was saying! "Your son-in-law Ralph! He's trying to take over your farm and use the land for Dalton Stables. You can't want that!"

"Ralph is an idiot! He can't even sit a horse. Never should have let him marry our girl. Reba says Ralph will make a success of hisself, but I don't see it. Now Benjamin. There's a natural horseman!"

He'd brought his wife and his son back to life in his head. As much as I needed him to come back to the present, I couldn't blame him for being wherever he was. *A natural horseman.* Even Dotty had never told me that.

Almost before my head knew it, my heart was talking to God: *God, You are my only hope. I don't want to lose Orphan.* I looked at my grandfather frowning in concentration. *And I don't want to lose my grandfather either. Please take care of him.*

Then as if something unclogged inside me, things began breaking loose. I imagined Grandad lifted up to God. Then everything else got unstuck, and I was giving God back what was His—Dotty, B.C., Orphan, me.

"It's time to sleep now," I said, pulling the faded quilt over Grandad. He leaned back in bed and let me tuck him in like I used to do B.C. "You get some rest and you'll feel better. Okay?"

He stared up at me, a light coming into his eyes, like a spring trickling up from the desert. I could tell he really saw me. "Scoop?"

"Yes, Grandad! It's me. Scoop." I felt tears fill my eyes and run over. I sat on the bed next to him. Watching his face was like seeing someone through the windshield wipers in the pouring rain. Every so often, the view would clear, only to blur over again, as if nothing had ever cleared.

He was crying. "Where am I, Scoop?" He sounded like a little boy. "There are no smells here, Scoop. I want to go home. Tell Reba to come and get me." He was sobbing.

I smoothed the sides of his hair down and put my arm around his shoulder. "It's okay. Don't cry. Please, don't cry."

Suddenly he jumped up from the bed and shoved me away. He pulled a little suitcase from under B.C.'s bed and started throwing things out—socks, papers, cigars. Then he got still, reached into the back pocket of the suitcase and pulled out some folded white papers.

He clutched them to his heart and glanced around the room. Then he crooked his finger at me to come closer. When I did, he handed the papers to me quickly, as if we were spies in the middle of a secret mission. "Now git," he said, crawling back in bed and under the covers.

I backed out of the room and pulled the door shut. I took the secret papers to the window, where the moon shone bright enough to read by. Slowly I unfolded the stack of papers in my hands. Holding the bundle up to the moonlight, I read the front: *Last Will and Testament of Jared B. Coop.*

11

I stayed up half the night trying to make sense out of Grandad's will. It gave me the creeps. I'd never seen anybody's will before. And even though Grandad wasn't sick, not that way, I was convinced he'd given me that will in one of his clear moments and I had to find out why.

About 1:00 A.M., Dotty had come out to see why the light was on. We studied the will together until I guess I fell asleep. When I woke up, it was Wednesday morning, and I was in my own bed. I got dressed fast and stumbled downstairs, feeling half asleep.

Dotty, in full Hy-Klas uniform, had a cup of coffee in one hand and the will in the other.

"Scoop!" she said. "I was coming up to wake you. I've been talking on the phone all morning to Mr. Ford's son, the lawyer. He's real smart. And I think I figured out why your grandaddy gave this here to you, Honey."

We sat at the table, and Dotty pointed out something on page three. I read it, but it was loaded with *whereas* and *party of the second parts*.

Benjamin Coop's name was all through it. "Just tell me what it means!" I begged, frustrated. I felt like my brain was coated with fuzz. "Is it going to help me keep Orphan?"

A shadow passed over Dotty's face. "I can't rightly say, Scoop. We have to trust God with that. Mr. Ford's son says the will don't count for much yet. But your grandad wants, or wanted, to leave land to both his kin. Patricia gets Dalton Stables, although that one's like closing the barn door after the horse is out since her and Ralph have already done taken it over. But your dad, Benjamin Coop, shoulda got the horse farm."

I felt my heart sink. "So what? He should have gotten the farm, but he didn't. What good does that do *me* now?"

"You and B.C. are your dad's next-of-kin, his heirs," Dotty said.

"Are you saying the farm could go to us?" The idea was too wild to even think about. "B.C. and I could own the land? And Orphan could stay there? And Moby! And who knows what other horses we might take in, horses that need a home? Dotty, you know I've always dreamed of running a home for backyard horses. I just never thought I'd need it this soon."

I could picture the whole thing though—people bringing problem horses for me to love and gentle. We'd be just like those girls in the war Jen read about, the ones who gentled horses everybody else had given up on. "Dotty, this is so great—"

"Now don't go getting too excited," Dotty said. "There's a lot standing betwixt you and that there farm. And it ain't just Ralph and Patricia Dalton neither. The land was only to go to your dad *if* he'd proved hisself responsible enough to run it."

"That sounds like Grandad," I said. "How would he have proved Dad was responsible?"

Dotty gulped her coffee, made a face, then set down the empty cup. "By keeping up the payments on the farm, for one thing."

Payments. We were back to that again. "Stephen's dad said Grandad owed the bank. He said if Grandad doesn't make his payments by the first of the month, they'll foreclose on him— or the Daltons will buy him out."

"That's true enough," Dotty said. "I found the papers in your grandad's things." She shoved over a notice, written in red.

"That's what he owes?" I asked. "That's three times our rent here. Where would I get that kind of money?"

Dotty glanced at her watch. "Goodness! I've got to go! I ain't been late to work in seven years, and I ain't about to start now." She yelled into her bedroom, "B.C.! We're leaving!" Dotty kissed the top of my head. "Scoop, don't you forget to thank God for bringing back Orphan yesterday. We can trust Him with the rest."

I skipped breakfast and left Grandad a note. Dotty said she'd check in on him during the day. I was too anxious to see Orphan to stick around another minute.

Geese honked overhead as I made my way through the morning light to Grandad's barn. I looked up in time to see them switch leaders and straighten their V-formation.

Orphan's stall was empty, and for a split second I gave in to all the despair of the day before. But she came running in from the pasture when I called, tossing her head in a playful, welcoming wave.

Since I didn't have Punch and Judy to groom, I got to spend extra time with Orphan. I jumped on her back and sat there for a few minutes while she grazed lazily on green clover in the pasture. I stroked her withers and talked to her, her ears flicking back to pick up my chatter about Grandad, my dad the natural horseman, and the will. The rest of the pasture looked abandoned. I missed the 2-year-olds, and I think Orphan did too.

I left Orphan with extra oats and tried to brush off the little black hairs that clung to my jeans as I walked to school.

Maggie and Jen were waiting for me by the main doors. "Everybody knows why you ran out yesterday," Maggie said. "It must have been awful to think Orphan was sold. I gave Stephen Dalton a piece of my mind."

"She sure did," Jen said. "You should have been there, Scoop. A masterful performance."

Ray joined us, and I filled them all in on the will, the bank, the due date, and some of the stuff about Grandad. "So, any ideas how I can come up with that much money in 10 days?"

"How much does everybody have?" Maggie asked, reaching into her bright red purse, which matched everything she wore today—short red skirt, silky red blouse, red sandals. "I've got $8 on me, and maybe $35 more in the bank. I've been saving it for violin lessons. It's not much, but it's all yours, Scoop."

I didn't know what to say. Then I remembered Maggie's own horse problem. "But what about you, Maggie?" I asked. "What have you worked out for Moby?"

Maggie sighed dramatically. "Mother said yes to Mr. Chesley. They're getting married next month. We'll move into his house with his bratty kids. But he said he'd pay to board Moby at Dalton Stables. He's really nice and everything, and I'm happy for my mom. But I feel like I'm sending Moby away to prison."

Moby would hate it at Dalton Stables, cooped up with show horses that wouldn't give her the time of day. But at least Maggie could keep her horse. "Thanks, Maggie," I said. I knew that Maggie's money wouldn't get me any closer to saving Orphan and the farm, but it felt good to have her offer.

"I've got about $20 in baby-sitting money, and I'll get $15 from Granny next month for my birthday. You can have that," Jen offered.

"I have exactly $11.50," Ray said, thumbing through his wallet. "But I owe Travis five, and five of it's my mom's because I have to pick up milk on the way home. Sorry. I'm baling hay at Harper's this weekend. You can have whatever I earn from that."

I couldn't even look them in the eyes. I bit my lip and stared down at the grass breaking through a crack in the sidewalk. "Thanks."

"But she'll need a *lot* more money than that," Jen said.

The bell rang, and we followed the noisy stream of students inside, then broke off to homeroom. I hardly even noticed Carla or wondered about Carl. I had enough to worry about without them.

School dragged on, and the day grew hotter and muggier. Even teachers glanced more often at the big, white wall clocks, urging the hands to jerk faster toward the end of class.

After school I walked to the farm. I had to pass the Hy-Klas. B.C. waved at me to join him on the roof. I climbed the back fire escape and sat beside him in the shade of the overhanging oak tree. It was hard to sit on that roof and not think about the talk Dotty and I had there years ago.

"I want you to have this," B.C. said, pulling something from inside his sock. When he lifted up his pantleg, I saw that his socks didn't match. They were both white, but one reached halfway up his calf and had three green stripes at the top. "Maybe this will help you buy Orphan, Scoop."

I looked at the plastic Baggie filled with pennies. "Where did you get these, B.C.?"

He grinned. "I sold some of my bottle cap figures," he said. "Just a few. Mr. Ford bought one."

I hugged my brother and said an inside prayer of thanks for him. "Thanks, B.C.," I told him. "You're the best."

Orphan was waiting for me when I reached the barn. I was walking through her stall to meet her in the pasture when I spotted a note tacked to her stall door. It said: "Scoop—Meet me at the south pasture. Bring Orphan. I know how you can get the money you need!" And it was signed "Carl."

I tried not to get my hopes up as I rode Orphan to meet Carl. A horsefly buzzed around my head, and I swatted at it. Jen's homemade elixir protected Orphan from fly attacks, but not me. We trotted, but the buzz stuck with me like the hum of conscience.

The south pasture lay hidden by a row of hedgeapple trees. I hadn't been back there for ages. Carl wasn't there yet. When I looked around, I was surprised to see the old arena still standing in the middle of the field. The wooden ring slanted east, as if someone had leaned against it.

I've never seen the sense of riding around in a circle, practicing for shows in an arena, when there are so many dirt roads and back fields to ride in.

My grandfather had built the arena for his kids. But Patricia didn't like horses, and Benjamin, my dad, didn't like shows any more than I do.

I urged Orphan to the arena's open gate.

The post moved when I touched it. Grass smelled different here, thicker somehow, with a heavy sweetness. Inside the ring, the green covering grew slightly shorter than outside, as if it remembered horses had trampled its ground once.

I felt Orphan tense beneath me. She arched her neck, pricked her ears toward the west, and let out a loud, long whinny. I squinted at the horizon, staring ahead, as if her pointed ears were sights.

Over the ridge with a backdrop of pure blue sky came a prancing horse that had to be Buckingham's British Pride. As they got closer, I saw Carl sitting on an English saddle, probably one I'd seen that first day. They looked like the cover for *Horse Magazine*. Carl sat straight, posting up and down like a wind-up toy. He wore a black hard hat, black sweats, and a black sweatshirt. He pulled up next to us, with Ham stretching out his front legs like horses in the show ring. Ham and Orphan snorted at each other, smelling their hellos.

"Not bad," I said, looking up at him, since Ham must have been nearly 17 hands high.

Carl seemed to size up Orphan and me. He clicked at Ham, making the sound at the side of his mouth. Then he rode slowly all the way around me while Orphan stood still. "Good," he said, nodding approvingly.

I didn't like the feeling of being judged, another reason I hate horse shows. "Come on, Carl," I said. "Your note? Remember? What's this big money-making idea?"

"Rats!" he said. "I forgot to tell you to bring your saddle."

I looked down at the weeds growing up all around the arena. I didn't have a saddle. Neither did Orphan. In fact, the only time I'd sat a saddle was on Jen's Western after her horse threw Mr. Zucker. I hadn't wanted Cheyenne to get away with it, so I got back on her.

"Orphan and I don't much like saddles," I said, not looking at him.

"Well, from now on, bring it anyway," he said.

I was getting irritated the more embarrassed I felt. What was it to him if I didn't have a saddle? "Yeah, yeah, so you want to get to the point, Carl? What's this big idea of yours?"

Carl leaned back in the saddle and grinned. Then he pulled out a horse show poster for the West Salem County Horse Show. "I can't believe we didn't think of it before, Scoop!" he said. "Did you know about this?"

I knew. Every year the county held a fair and horse show at the West Salem County Fairgrounds. I never paid that much attention. I took the horse show poster from Carl's outstretched hand and read what Carl had circled:

Grand Prize Giveaway sponsored by Dalton Stables—$500.

"Isn't that just too great?" Carl was talking so fast, I had to piece together the words, filling in the ones I couldn't understand. "Five hundred dollars, Scoop! I know what you're going to say. I know Mr. Dalton is just doing this for publicity now that he thinks he'll get land to expand Dalton Stables. But so what? Scoop, think about it! With that prize money, and your horse fund savings, you could pay off the bank! And the prize money won't be divided up either. It all goes for first prize in the last class, the Pleasure Horse Class, English Pleasure."

I stared at Carl on his high-class horse and fancy saddle. His leather boots looked like Stephen's, tall and expensive. "You still don't get it, do you, Carl? I can't ride in that horse show. That's for people like you—and Stephen Dalton—not people like me."

"Don't be silly, Scoop. I've seen you ride. You're terrific!"

"You've seen me ride bareback. I can't ride with a saddle. I don't have a saddle." My face felt hot, and my whole body quivered with shame. "I've never even sat on an English saddle, Carl. That money might as well be a grand prize for quilt-making!"

Carl didn't say anything. Around us crows cawed. A squirrel jumped to a lower branch, making it snap.

Finally Carl spoke. "You're wrong, Scoop. I can teach you. You can learn. This is only Wednesday. The show's a week from Saturday. We can do this! So what if you don't have a saddle? You can use one of our saddles."

A week from Saturday—just in time to pay off Grandad's mortgage payment. I felt a sprout of hope inside me. It could mean keeping Orphan and the barn. Five hundred dollars would go a long way. What if I ...?

But I didn't know how to ride English. I shook the notion out of my head. "Carl, there's no way—" An idea flashed in my mind, a replay of Carl and Ham prancing on the horizon. "Unless ... Carl, *you* do it! I mean, Stephen's the odds-on favorite, but you could actually—"

I stopped. Carl's whole expression had dissolved. He wouldn't look at me.

"What is it?" I asked. Then I understood. "It's Carla, isn't it? You won't get to ride in the horse show because of her. *She's* riding Ham. That's it, isn't it! She won't let you ride."

Carl didn't deny it.

"It's not fair!" I cried. "Carla gets everything! I ought to ride over there right now and tell your mother—"

"Don't!" Carl sounded desperate, scared. "Promise me you won't talk to anybody about me. You don't understand."

"*You* don't understand, Carl! Do you know that Carla told our whole class she didn't have a brother? You call that fair? She thinks she's better than everybody else!" I wanted him to get mad at her, as mad as I was.

Carl shook his head. "You don't know Carla, Scoop. She'd give you the money herself if she won, but our mother would never allow it."

"Carla, give *me* the prize money? Sure she would," I said sarcastically. "Tell you what—Let's settle this right now." I was shouting, and Orphan didn't like it. She sidestepped nervously and jostled into Ham. "Let's ride over to Buckingham Palace and ask Carla *and* your mom how they feel about all this. I'd love to have it out with both of them!" I neck-reined Orphan so she pivoted away.

"Scoop! If you try to talk to my mother or to anyone else about me, I'm out of here." Carl's voice got softer. "I mean it. I can't ride in the horse show for you or I would. But I'll coach you every night. And I think you have a chance to win the money yourself. My only condition is that nobody finds out about me."

Ham had picked up Carl's tension and was dancing around, lifting one hoof high, then the other. Carl looked more determined than I'd ever seen him. A quiet strength wrapped around him like a horse blanket. I knew it wouldn't do a bit of good to argue.

"You honestly think you could make me good enough to win that Pleasure Class? You really think I have a chance?" It was crazy. Stephen had won that show every single year for as long as I could remember. No wonder the Daltons put up the prize money. They'd be sure to keep it in the family.

"We'll have to work every day after school," Carl said. "I won't kid you. This isn't going to be easy. But yes, I think you have a chance. You're a natural, Scoop. I know how to ride because I've had a million lessons. But you—you just connect with horses. I've never seen anything like it."

Carl lifted Ham's reins and moved in closer to Orphan and me. "I'm only asking for one thing, Scoop—that you keep our bargain and don't tell anybody about me. If you do, I'm out of here. So, is it a deal?"

I leaned forward on Orphan's withers and scratched her as high on the neck as I could reach. It wasn't much of a chance, but it was the only one I had. "You've got a deal."

"We've got a lot of work to do," Carl said. "We might as well get started." He smoothly dismounted the puny English saddle, unbuckled a couple of buckles, slid the stirrup up and slipped the saddle off with one arm. Then he tilted his head, motioning me to get off too.

I swung my right leg up and over Orphan's withers so I was sitting side-saddle, only without the saddle. Then I dropped to the ground only a foot from where Carl was standing.

Carl pressed his lips together so he wouldn't grin. He pointed to the flat English saddle over his arm. "This," he announced, "is a saddle."

I acted shocked.

"Maybe I'm going too fast," Carl said. "Let's just start with the saddle blanket. He passed me the saddle-shaped, navy blanket, slightly larger than the saddle.

I took it, turned, and flung the saddle blanket up on Orphan. "No problem," I said.

Orphan twitched, then crooked her head all the way around, grabbed the saddle blanket in her teeth, and threw it to the ground.

Carl chuckled. "Looks like we have our work cut out for us."

13

Thursday afternoon Carl and Ham were waiting at the arena for Orphan and me. All day in school I'd wanted to tell Maggie and Jen about Carl, but I kept my promise and kept my mouth shut.

Carl waved as we entered the field. He dismounted and took off his black hard hat. Underneath, he was wearing a Dodgers baseball cap.

As soon as Carl unsaddled Ham, I felt Orphan get all spooky. "I know, Girl," I murmured. "I feel the same way about that saddle."

The flies were bad, but I'd used Jen's homemade fly spray, and Orphan was fly-free. I'd even dabbed a bit of the stuff on my jeans and tee-shirt. It helped. Ham, on the other hand, twitched, swatted with his tail, and shook his head to keep off the flies. "Next time I'll bring fly wipe for Ham," I said. "Jen's secret formula." I slid off Orphan.

"Great," Carl said. "Just don't tell her it's for me though, okay?" He held out Ham's English saddle to me. "You can use this one. Ham and I will watch."

I stared at the saddle, its dark leather stiffer, newer, more expensive-looking than the one Carl had used before. "Horsefeathers, Carl. I can't use that saddle." I tried to hand it back to him.

"Sure you can, Scoop," he insisted. "We have more saddles at home."

"But that's got to be your best saddle. Carla will freak if she sees me with it. I don't want to get you in trouble."

"Let me worry about that, okay? We don't have time to argue." Carl shoved the saddle at me, the blanket on top.

I was discovering how hard it was to argue with him. Resigned, I looped Orphan's reins around the fence, which never would have held her if she'd wanted to bolt. When I picked up the saddle, I was surprised how light it felt. The leather smelled like cooked cherries and forest, and I took a deep breath before flinging the saddle on Orphan.

I knew enough to reach underneath and buckle the russet leather girth. Orphan didn't even budge. "That was easy," I said, brushing my hands on my jeans.

Carl grinned. "Orphan's cheating on you, Scoop."

"What are you talking about?" I asked.

Carl walked to Orphan's head. "Check this out." He lifted Orphan's top lip. She had her pink tongue pressed against her teeth all the way around.

"She's smart," Carl said. "She's holding her breath so you can't get the saddle tight. She'll let out her breath when you're not looking. Then when you try to get on, the saddle will slip, and you'll land on your keister."

"Horsefeathers, Orphan!" I said, tickling her belly. I heard a rush of air as she let out her breath. I pulled the saddle strap three notches tighter.

"We'll just tack up with the saddle today," Carl said. "We'll save the English bridle for another day." I'd forgotten English bridles were different—four reins instead of two. As usual, all Orphan had on was a hackamore, a training bridle with no bit. That bridle business would be tough on both of us.

"Mount up!" Carl commanded.

Orphan craned her neck around and nudged me when I tried to get on. I wasn't stupid about saddles. I knew you mount from the left side. Still, I didn't quite feel ready to stick my boot into that little metal stirrup. So I stalled.

"Know why we mount from the left side?" I asked. "Jen says horses have two brains, not just two sides of the brain like we do. So just because you get a horse used to something on his left side, doesn't mean he's going to like it on his right. It's kind of like he's two horses."

Carl stopped what he was doing. "Two horses?"

"Well, that's what Jen says, and she knows a lot about it."

"Scoop," Carl said, idly stroking Orphan's neck. "Do you ever feel like you're two people?"

"Nope." I said it quickly and laughed. But then I thought about how I felt when I was riding Orphan—like I could do or be anything I wanted to be. An Indian princess. When I was at school it was different. *I* was different, like a different person. "Well, kind of, maybe," I said.

"So do I, Scoop. So do I." Carl changed as suddenly as a shift in the wind. "Okay, you two! Now mount up and get in that arena. Not like that, Scoop. Put one hand on the pommel," he instructed, "and the other hand there, on the cantle."

Somehow I pulled myself up in spite of the saddle.

"We'll have to work on mounting later," Carl said. He tossed me his black riding helmet and made me buckle it under my chin. I felt like I was inside a conch shell, like the ones Maggie brought back from her vacation by the sea.

Orphan and I did as we were told, but Orphan didn't like the arena any more than I did. She kept bumping into the fence, rubbing against it, trying to get the saddle or me off.

Carl stood in the middle with Ham and shouted out riding tips: "You need a saddle horse seat, Scoop! Think—balanced seat! ... Keep your eyes forward."

My right foot slipped out of the metal stirrup. I couldn't get it back in. I leaned over and grabbed the stirrup, pushing my toe deep through it.

"Keep the stirrup irons under the balls of your feet!" Carl yelled. "Hey, heels down, remember?"

Around and around the arena we went, in the same boring circles. "Back straight!" Carl hollered. "No, not that straight! Relax!"

There was no relaxing going on. Orphan and I walked and trotted, then walked and cantered in the ring. If I did something right, I'd forget and do something else wrong.

Finally I pulled Orphan out of the circular path. "Carl," I said, "I'm getting dizzy. I have got to get out of this arena!"

"But you need to practice—"

"We need a break," I hollered, willing Orphan out of the gate and letting her have her head. We cantered to the top of the pasture. *One, two, three, pause*. In that fourth beat of the canter, all hooves are off the ground. We were flying or floating, the breeze whipping Orphan's mane in my face when I leaned forward over her withers.

She flicked her ears up and back and let out a playful kick. It was the most fun we'd had all day.

I let Orphan pick our path, and she raced to the foot of the field, where trees dropped gifts at her hooves—apples, walnuts, spinning maple wings. After zigzagging across the pasture, we turned and trotted back to Carl. I bounced all over the place and might have bounced right off if I hadn't grabbed a lock of mane to steady me.

Carl was leaning against the arena, one boot crossed over the other. Ham stood quietly, looking left out and longing.

"Boy, do you need to practice posting, Scoop!" Carl shouted, laughing so hard I could barely understand him. "If you're done goofing off, you two, I'd thank you to get back in that wonderful arena. And just for a change of pace, go clockwise this time."

"Wow, Orphan," I said, my voice flat, "won't that be fun." But I walked her into the ring.

"Huh-uh," Carl hollered, taking up his position in the center of the arena again. "Teee—rrot! Let's see that trot. That's it, Orphan! Scoop! Post. Up and down! Up, down. Feel the rhythm with Orphan as she moves."

"Horsefeathers, Carl!" I griped. "How am I supposed to feel Orphan with this stinking saddle between us?" My voice came out as bumpy as the ride.

After another hour of circles, we called it a day and agreed to meet the same time the next day.

~~~~~~~~~~~~~~~~~~~~~~~~~~~~~~~

If anything, Friday's practice went even worse than Thursday's. I rode about the same—awful. But on Friday Orphan started messing up too. She kept taking the wrong lead. Carl explained that he could see it—Orphan's outside foreleg and hind leg leading off in the canter, instead of the other way around. Every time we broke from a walk to a canter, Orphan stuck out her outer legs first. I had trouble seeing the missed lead, but I could sure feel it. Instead of Orphan's normal canter, which was so smooth I could sip a glass of water without spilling, the wrong-lead gait felt like she was hobbling over walnuts. It jarred me almost as much as the trot.

We practiced hard after that and scheduled two practices for Saturday. I told Carl all about my plans for the prize money—turning the Coop Barn into a home for backyard horses, where they could be free to be horses. Maggie and Jen had heard about my horse dream, but I'd never shared it with anybody else. Carl listened and said he thought it was a super idea. But he still didn't open up or talk much about himself. And whenever I tried to ask him anything about Carla or his family, he shut me down.

It was near the end of our Saturday morning workout when something seemed to click in. It was like a boot you've been tugging and tugging on and it finally slips on just right. Even Carl looked pleased with Orphan and me and maybe a little surprised. He only yelled instructions at us about half as much as the day before.

"I don't know, Scoop," he said as I led Orphan around the paddock to cool her down. "You looked really good posting out there today."

"Yeah?" I asked. But I'd felt it too. I'd almost felt like Carl in the arena, with my chin up and the rest of me going up and down, up and down, matching Orphan's stride.

I led Orphan to the cross-ties and started brushing her moist coat. Carl helped me rub her down.

Neither of us said anything for a couple of minutes. Then Carl started to say something, then stopped. He tried again. "Scoop?" he said, working on one side of Orphan, with me on the opposite side. "Something I've been meaning to ask you. How did you first figure out about twins?"

"It wasn't that hard," I said. "I saw *Carl* marked on some of the boxes when you guys were moving in. Then I saw *Carla* on others. You both had boxes marked *8th Grade*. So I just put two and two together and came up with twins—same year, and your names are so much alike."

This was the first time Carl had brought up anything this close to home. I had to take advantage of it and see if I could get him talking. "You know, Carl," I said, trying to sound casual, "you and Carla can't keep pretending you don't exist."

Carl got quiet on me.

I tried again. "I mean, it's not like I'm going to tell on you or anything—you know I won't do that. I know it's no big deal to miss the last couple of weeks of school. But what about next year? You're going to have to straighten everybody out—like Mrs. Gopher and the principal and everybody."

Carl moved back and brushed Orphan's long, black tail. I picked off fly eggs, tiny yellow specks, from Orphan's red-tinged neck.

"Maggie and Jen would really like to meet you, Carl," I said. "So would Ray. You'll like Ray. I think he's got a crush on Carla—don't ask me why."

"He does?" Carl asked, his mouth twisting into a grin.

I shrugged. "But he would really like to meet you too." Truth was, I didn't even know if Ray believed me about Carl. If I could only get the two of them together ... "I was thinking of asking the guys to come watch us practice."

Carl shook his head so hard his Texas Rangers cap almost fell off. "Scoop," he said. "These practices are between you and me. Nobody else. We have an agreement."

"Horsefeathers," I muttered. "I know." But inside I was thinking that our agreement stank. And I wasn't sure how long I could keep it.

14

Saturday evening we met back at the arena for our second workout of the day. The sun was still high, and a half-moon hung directly opposite the orange ball. Orphan acted as frisky and spry as if I hadn't ridden her for a month. Carl had Ham on a halter and let him graze while Orphan and I did the work. He had us canter in one direction, reverse, and canter again. Over and over, we did the same routine.

"You've got it!" Carl shouted, giving us a little applause. "Orphan knows which lead to take. She hasn't missed a lead the last seven tries!"

"Good!" I called back. "I thought it felt right." The cantering had been smooth, *one, two, three, four.* But it still didn't feel like flying, not like when we'd galloped outside the arena.

We practiced another hour, and Orphan only missed leads twice.

"I've about had it for today," Carl said. "Bring Orphan into the center and line her up."

I rode my mare in next to Ham as straight as we could get. I touched Orphan's shoulders with the tip of my boots, and she stretched, not as far down as Ham, but not bad.

Carl acted like a horse show judge. He walked slowly all the way around us, stopping as if he were taking stock of confirmation, jotting notes on an invisible pad. "Don't look at me," he said when I turned my head just a fraction of an inch. "Stare straight between Orphan's ears."

I stared through Orphan's ears toward the grove of hedgeapple trees. The sun was nearing the horizon now, rippling the sky with pink and purple stripes. Finally, Carl ordered me to dismount and unsaddle my horse.

"Not a bad dismount," Carl said when I touched ground. "Why don't you unsaddle her here? I'll put it on Ham and we can lead them in for their cooling off period."

I unbuckled the girth while Carl held Orphan. I wanted to ask Carl something that had been on my mind all afternoon. "Carl, is Carla really as good as everybody says? I mean, is she as big a worry to me in the horse show as Stephen Dalton?"

Carl looked embarrassed. "She's won a lot of trophies."

"Well why does she have to show off here in our dinky town?"

Carl rushed to her defense as usual. "Mother makes her show in every show on the circuit. She tracks points. Carla really doesn't have a choice, Scoop."

"I'll bet," I said.

Carl looked so hurt I wished I hadn't said it. But it drove me nuts the way he always stuck up for his sister. I figured belonging in a real family must make you overlook a lot. And somehow that made me even madder.

I had Orphan's saddle off and was reaching for the blanket when I changed my mind. "I'm going to work a little longer," I said. If Carla was half as good as Carl thought she was, I needed all the practice I could get.

"But we're done, Scoop. We already did two workouts," Carl argued.

I hoisted the saddle back up on Orphan. She craned her neck and gave me a surprised and disapproving look. "I only have one week," I said. "I don't feel like stopping."

"Listen, Scoop," Carl pleaded. "You and Orphan have come a long way. You're doing fine. Don't push it."

"I *have* to push it!" I snapped.

"Well I think we've all had enough for today," Carl insisted.

"No." I mounted Orphan and reined her to the rail. "Go ahead. Call out gaits." We took the rail at a trot.

Carl sighed, but he took his position in the

center of the arena. He acted as ringmaster for another half hour, while dark shadows descended on the ring and frogs and crickets began their night bickering.

Orphan missed two leads in a row.

"She's tired, Scoop!" Carl called out, his arms stretched out from his sides. From where I sat on Orphan, he looked like a scarecrow. "We can work on this Monday. There's a time when you have to trust yourself and your horse."

Trust myself? Trust my horse? Dotty would have added trust God.

"I can't!" I cried. I felt a desperation growing in me. I imagined Carla and Ham prancing perfectly around the ring. I knew Orphan was tired. The sweat at her neck and under the saddle had turned to white foam. I was tired too. But I couldn't stop, especially not now when she was missing leads. If she missed just one lead in the horse show, I'd be out.

I reversed Orphan. "Call out the canter!" I commanded.

"No!" Carl yelled. "It's getting too dark."

It was still bright enough. The half-moon was almost up and Venus and the North Star shone with a strong, white light that flooded the arena. "Do it, Carl!"

"No. I'm leaving, Scoop. I should have been home over an hour ago. So should you." He turned to go.

"Go then!" I shouted.

Carl picked up Ham's lead rope and led him away. "Monday after school then," he called. He turned around, but I couldn't see the expression on his face. "Scoop, please stop for tonight."

"I can't, Carl! I'm sorry I yelled at you. You go on. I'll come in a minute. I just want Orphan to get that left lead a couple of times before I quit."

"Are you sure?" he asked.

"I'm sure. Go! I'll see you Monday." I watched the darkness swallow up Carl and Ham. Fireflies blinked on and off all around them and across the pasture, like tiny, twinkling stars in a lower sky.

"Come on, Orphan." I nudged her to a trot. Up and down. I could feel the rhythm for posting now without too much trouble. Then I slowed her to a walk. I felt her muscles tense. She knew what was coming, and she wanted to please me. "Canter," I whispered. I squeezed my thighs in and concentrated on the movement.

Orphan picked up on my signal and broke into a nice, easy gait that I knew must be the correct lead. Her canter grew more intense, a little faster than Carl liked us to go. One lap around. I'd let her canter one more lap to make sure she remembered the feel of that lead.

Enough light streamed down from the sky

for me to see the arena all the way around, although I couldn't actually make out the ground any longer. Orphan's hooves beat the one, two, three, glide rhythm, padding into the dirt. *One, two, three, glide. One, two—*

Orphan's head jerked down. I lunged forward in the saddle, catching myself with a hand to her neck. I felt my horse crumble, as if her forelegs were nothing more than cardboard. She bowed, stumbled, and fell to her knees. My feet jerked out of the stirrups, and I was hurled into the air. I flew over Orphan's head and saw weeds and ground rushing toward me. With a jolt, I landed on my elbow and hip, then flopped to my back.

For a minute I lay there, looking up at stars and wondering if they were real. I couldn't breathe. White splotches swarmed in front of me, as if someone had snapped a flash bulb in my face.

Then my breath came back. I inhaled. The air smelled bitter. Slowly I sat up and felt my elbow, which stung like fire. Gritty dirt, covered with blood came off on my fingers. But I could bend my arm. Stiff, but not broken. *Thank You, Lord,* I muttered.

Orphan was standing over me, her head inches from mine. I reached up and stroked her jaw, wincing from the pain in my arm. "I'm okay, Girl," I said. "You sure gave me a scare, though."

When I got to my feet, I reminded myself of Grandad getting up from the TV recliner. Each joint had to be stretched individually, with grunts and groans.

Orphan still hadn't moved. I picked up the reins and led her toward the pasture. She took one step and hobbled, throwing her weight off her left foreleg.

My heart chilled. "Orphan?" I said, turning toward her. Even in the pale moonlight, I could see pain in her eyes. Facing her, I pulled her forward again. She limped, keeping the left foreleg stiff.

Tears broke loose, and I started to shake. What had I done to her? I threw my arms around her neck and buried my face in her sweat. "Orphan," I cried, over and over. "I'm sorry. It's all my fault." Why couldn't I have quit when Carl did? I had done this to her.

I wanted to carry her back to the barn. I walked the whole way with my arm over her withers. Every step, every limp, was like a hammer driving a stake through my heart. Orphan was in pain because of me.

15

From the pasture, Grandad's barn appeared as a golden glow through the night fog. I didn't remember leaving the lights on, but I was relieved to see them. My head hurt from studying the ground in front of Orphan, trying to make sure she didn't step in a hole or on anything that could hurt her even more.

As soon as we entered the paddock, I heard my name. "Scoop! Scoop!" Carl came running out of the barn. "What happened? What's wrong?"

I started crying again and couldn't answer him.

He ran up and stared at me, then at Orphan. "I got all the way home," he said, slurring his words worse than ever, running them into each other. "But I was worried about you. I came back. You weren't here. Are you okay? Your arm—what happened to it?"

Carl reached for my arm, but I jerked it away. It stung now, and I saw I'd scraped it worse than I'd thought. "I didn't get hurt," I said. "It's ... it's Orphan."

"What's the matter with Orphan?" Carl squinted at her.

"It's all my fault," I said, sniffing back tears. "I should have quit. I should have left when you did. Orphan stepped in something or tripped—I don't know. But she's hurt, Carl. I think it's bad. She's limping something awful."

"Let me see," Carl said. He took the reins and led Orphan a few paces toward the barn. Her limp hadn't gotten any better. Carl smoothed his hand down Orphan's leg the way he had the first day I met him, when Orphan had picked up a rock in the frog of her hoof. But this was different. This time Orphan's pain wasn't something we could take out with a stick.

"Let's get her in the barn," Carl said, leading the way. He glanced back at me as I followed Orphan and him into the glow of the barn. Once inside, Carl said, "Don't look so worried, or guilty, Scoop. Orphan will be okay. She's putting some weight on the bad leg, so that's a good sign. A week's a long time. She'll probably be fine by the horse show."

A week. The horse show. I'd completely forgotten. "I won't make Orphan enter that horse show," I said, "not if she's like this." It was the stupid horse show that had gotten us into this mess. I stroked Orphan's blaze and prayed she'd be okay. "I'm not leaving her until I know she's okay," I said.

Carl took a minute before talking again. "I'll go home and call the vet. You stay with Orphan."

I nodded. It would have taken more than all the king's horses and all the king's men to tear me away from my horse.

Carl ran out of the barn, leaving Orphan and me by ourselves. I brushed her gently, while moths flapped around the bare light bulb above us. Over and over again, I told her how sorry I was. Frogs croaked from the pond. Crickets droned. Orphan didn't nicker or snort or make a sound.

After maybe a half hour, I heard a car door slam, then a second door. "Scoop!"

"Maggie?" I called, wondering if it could really be her voice.

In walked Maggie 37 Brown. "Scoop!" she exclaimed, running toward me. "I knew it! Are you okay? You look awful!"

"But what are you—?" I started.

"I was at the vet's, Scoop, picking up Moby's worming medicine. The phone rang. As soon as I heard Doc Vicki say 'Coop's Barn,' I knew something awful had happened. Your arm's bleeding. Are you sure you're all right?" She held my wrist and studied my forearm.

"It's just a scrape," I said, wincing.

Vicki Snyder, the local veterinarian, came in, her black bag in one hand and her purse in the other. Her sun-streaked auburn hair was tied back in a ponytail. I'd known her for five years, since she moved to West Salem and took over Doc Howden's business. Doc Snyder might have been a Thoroughbred if she'd been a horse— long and kind of delicate-looking, but loaded with speed and power and endurance.

"Scoop," Doc said, "are you all right? You look a hundred times worse than Orphan." She wore an army shirt with rolled-up sleeves that showed all the muscles her slender arms could hold.

"I'm okay," I said, although my arm was getting stiff and hard to bend, and my hip felt like an elephant had stepped on it.

Doc set down the leather doctor's bag and stood in front of Orphan, looking into her eyes with a tiny flashlight. "It's a good thing Maggie was in the office. I almost wrote off the call as a crank. Caller wouldn't leave a name, and the voice was all muffled."

"I told her we *had* to check it out," Maggie said, trying to look over Doc's shoulder. "Some-body must have seen you fall. Is that what hap-pened, Scoop? Did you fall? Why were you riding in the dark anyway?"

"Hush now, Maggie," said Doc Vicki. She scratched Orphan's chin. "You can get your details later, okay? Scoop, I need you to tell me exactly what happened."

I swallowed hard to keep back tears as I went over the whole thing—the double workouts because of the horse show, the ride after dark, Orphan's tripping, the fall.

Maggie kept making little noises while I talked, like she was bursting to jump in, but doing everything she could to keep her mouth shut. Finally she exploded in a flurry of questions. "Scoop, why are you practicing for a horse show? And why didn't you tell me? Why are you so secretive? And why do you want to ride in the horse show anyway? I don't get it!"

"I imagine that prize money might have something to do with it?" Doc said, lifting Orphan's upper lip and shining a flashlight in her mouth. "Maggie was telling me your grandfather may have to sell the place if you can't come up with the money."

Maggie smiled sheepishly. "It just kind of came out, Scoop." Then she was back in my face. "Prize money? What prize money? How much is it? Is that why you're practicing for the horse show? Prize money?"

"Maggie 37," I said, "I'm awfully glad you're here, but you're wearing me out with questions."

"I'm sorry, Scoop." Maggie gave me a hug. Then little by little, I filled her in on the horse show and Dalton's prize giveaway.

Doc put her thumb on Orphan's jowl and reached her finger under her neck to take her respiration.

"But you don't know how to ride English, do you, Scoop? Why would you do this by yourself? Why didn't you tell me? Or Jen? We would have helped you."

Maggie looked so hurt. And she was right. She and Jen had been trying to help me all along. She'd run to my rescue, and here I was hurting her feelings, making her feel left out. I knew too well what that felt like.

I'd promised Carl I wouldn't tell anybody about him and I'd been keeping my promise. But Carl wasn't here, and Maggie was. And I couldn't stand hurting anybody else. "Maggie, I'm sorry. I wanted to tell you. I almost did a million times this week. It's just—"

Doc was studying her watch, still taking Orphan's pulse.

I whispered to Maggie, "It's Carl, Maggie. Carl's been helping me. He's been teaching me how to ride English—every day after school. He didn't want me to tell anybody. That's why I didn't tell you about the show or anything. Carl said he wouldn't help me if I told anyone."

"Carl?" Maggie said, like she didn't know whether to believe me or not. "Carl Buckingham has been helping you every day after school."

I nodded. "But he made me promise not to tell. So you have to promise not to say anything, Maggie. He's the one who called Doc."

"I guess that makes sense," Maggie said. "I still think it's stupid that he's hiding out like this. But if he can help you win that money, then I guess you have to play by his rules. Do you think—?"

Doc Vicki broke in. "Good!" she said, patting Orphan. "Twelve respirations per minute. Normal and steady. Let's take a look at that leg."

She led Orphan up and down the stallway. I glanced at Maggie. My stomach tightened and ached with every limping step. I held Orphan's lead rope while Doc examined every inch and hair of that foreleg. Finally she said, "Well, I'm glad you got me here right away, Scoop—even though I am standing up Mr. Tall, Dark, and Handsome."

"You should have seen this guy, Scoop," Maggie said. "He was waiting for Doc when I picked up the medicine. Talk about cute! He looked awfully disappointed when she told him she had an emergency."

It figured. Doc Vicki looked more like a New York model than what people around West Salem thought a vet should look like. It had taken her a couple of years to win over the farmers and breeders in the county. But now she was the first one people called when they needed help with their stock.

"I felt so sorry for him," Maggie said dramatically, "I almost offered to go out with him myself."

"I'm sorry, Doc Vicki," I said.

"No problem," said Doc. "He'll be back." Her eyes reminded me of a Morgan, a police horse that's seen it all but still cares. She'd been holding Orphan's hoof, and now she set it down gently. "I don't think Orphan sprained anything, Scoop," she said. "We'll know more in 24 hours, but I don't see any significant swelling."

Thank You, God, I said inside.

"What Orphan does have are contusions," said Doc, "bruising to her leg or joint. I think it's her cannon, just below her knee. Do you have a hose hooked up here?"

"I'll get it!" Maggie cried, running outside.

"We'll give your horse's leg a cold shower, Scoop. Then we'll follow up with some dry wraps. Now don't look like that," Doc said softly. "Orphan is going to be all right."

I nodded and stroked her head, feeling the guilt like fire in my throat.

Maggie ran in with the hose. We doused Orphan's leg, letting the cold water massage her cannon and pastern. Orphan didn't fight it. It tore at my heart to see her so listless, like she couldn't understand why I was letting all of this happen to her.

We dried the leg, and Doc brought out a tube and some elastic bandages. "Just to be on the safe side, we'll sweat her, okay?" Doc squeezed some of the ointment from the tube into her palm and rubbed it on Orphan's leg. "Maggie, run to the truck and get the Saran Wrap. It's under the passenger's seat."

Maggie came back with a fat roll of plastic wrap. Doc put it over the coating of ointment and wrapped Orphan's leg all the way around. She pulled a cotton pad out of her bag and put it over the plastic wrap.

"Scoop," Doc said, "I want you to take that elastic bandage there and wrap it over the pad while I hold it. Come on. Orphan and I don't have all day."

I knelt down and started to wind the light, brown bandage around Orphan's leg.

"I had to wrap my leg for cheerleading last year, remember, Scoop?" Maggie asked. "I used an Ace bandage just like that."

"Good, a little tighter though, Scoop," Doc said, tugging the elastic cloth to bring it flatter. "Now, a bandage like this, on the inside of the leg, needs to wrap forward, just like you're doing. That way, if Orphan bumps it with her right hoof, the bandage will tighten, instead of loosen."

I kept wrapping until the roll of elastic bandage was all wound around Orphan's cannon. Doc guided me in a couple of places, but kept telling me what a good job I was doing. I knew she was trying to make me feel better, and I appreciated it. But it wouldn't work. I'd never forgive myself for what I'd done to Orphan.

"That's it," Doc said, standing up and loading her bag again. "Not much more we can do for her, Scoop, except go home, get some sleep, and let Orphan do the same."

"How long before Scoop can ride Orphan again?" Maggie asked.

"I'm a vet, not a prophet," Doc Vicki said. "I'll drop by tomorrow evening and change the bandage. We'll see how she's doing then, okay?"

Doc gave Orphan a pat, then laid her hand on my head too. She headed for the truck.

"Doc?" I hollered after her. She turned around. "How ... I mean, I can't pay you tonight, but ... how much do I owe you?"

"Don't worry about it, Scoop. We'll work it out later. You say howdy to that aunt of yours. And get on home. Need a ride?"

I shook my head. "Thanks. I'll make sure Orphan's okay. It's a short walk home."

"See that she doesn't chew on the bandage, okay?" Doc said. "Maggie, how about you? Need a lift home?"

Maggie squeezed my hand. "Will you be okay, Scoop? I'll stay if you need me."

"Go!" I commanded. "It's late. Church tomorrow, remember?"

"Okay then." She ran after Doc Snyder. "I'm coming!"

I heard the truck doors slam and gravel churn as they drove off. Then I walked Orphan to her stall and stayed with her a while. Instead of taking her stall exit to the pasture like she always did, Orphan stayed inside. I pulled down some hay and filled her trough. Finally, I kissed her and walked home in darkness that seemed to sink into my soul.

16

Sunday before church I rode my bike down to the barn to check on Orphan. My stomach felt shaky when I saw Orphan's leg bandaged up. She hadn't touched the hay I'd left or gone out to graze. But she nickered when I walked in, as if even after all I'd done to her, she still loved me.

At church Jen Zucker ran up to me. "How's Orphan?" she whispered. "Maggie told me about the fall. Is she okay? I'm praying for her, Scoop. And you."

"Thanks, Jen," I said. For some reason, I felt like crying all over again.

"I wish Cheyenne were tamer," Jen said. "I'd enter that horse show too. Maybe one of us could win the money and pay off the bank."

I thanked her, but she'd already run off to catch up with one of the twins—Daniel, I think, but it might have been David. They were dressed exactly alike in black pants and light blue shirts.

I was relieved Jen hadn't mentioned Carl. Maybe Maggie realized how important it was for me to keep Carl secret, at least until after the horse show.

God must have known my limits and how close I was to them because both B.C. and Grandad were real good in church. Dotty didn't have charge of the nursery during main service, which was the first time in a long time. So all four of us—Dotty, B.C., Grandad, and me—sat in our pew just like regular, normal people.

Before the sermon got going, while we sang hymns I didn't have to look at the hymnal for, my mind kept flipping back to Orphan. The madder I got at myself, the madder I got at Carla, as if somehow her being such a good rider made me stay out practicing too long.

If I hadn't known better, I might have thought somebody had spilled everything, including all my thoughts, to our pastor. He talked about how Jesus died to forgive our sins, so we can forgive other people—and even forgive ourselves. I prayed God would help me do both.

~~~~~~~~~~~~~~~~~~~~~~~~~~~~~~~~~~

As soon as Dotty released me from our Sunday dinner, I changed clothes and spent the rest of the day hanging out with Orphan in her stall. I led her outside for a while to get fresh air and saw Maggie and Jen coming our way. They stayed for an hour and tried to cheer me up. Then they left for a ride.

B.C. brought sandwiches from Dotty and messed around on the barn roof before going back home. Orphan seemed to be limping less, and some of the sparkle had seeped back in her eyes.

Just like she'd promised, Doc Vicki showed up around dusk. I'd been sitting in a pile of hay, and I'd barely dozed off when I heard the door slam.

"So," Doc said, "how's the patient?" Doc looked so beautiful, it was a minute before I got my answer out. Her hair curled around her face, and she wore a sleek, black sleeveless dress that made her look like a movie star.

"Orphan's better, I think," I said. "You look great. Are you on your way somewhere?"

"As a matter of fact," she said, bending down to unwrap Orphan's bandage, "Tall, Dark, and Handsome is sitting out in the car even as we speak. But first things first, right?" She removed the entire bandage in a few seconds and felt the leg all over.

"Lead her around for me, Scoop," she said.

Doc watched as I led Orphan down the stall-way and back. Then she had me do it again.

"What do you think?" I asked, scared of her answer.

She sighed. "Well, let's put a new bandage on her tonight. I'll leave you some ointment, and you can change it again tomorrow. But unless she takes a turn for the worse, I don't need to see her again, Scoop. I doubt if you'll need the bandage more than a day or two. And as soon as she's not limping, you're safe to ride. Just take it easy at first. She's healing fast."

"Really?" I asked. "You're not just saying that?"

"I wouldn't be in business long if I just went around telling people their animals were fine." She watched while I applied the ointment and re-wrapped the leg. This time she didn't correct me even once.

"Scoop," she said, "have you ever thought about becoming a veterinarian?"

I shrugged. I'd thought about it. First I'd get my own stable for backyard horses. Then I'd get my veterinarian license. That's how the dream went.

"Too bad you're a female though," Doc said. "Girls can't be vets, you know." She laughed, but in a way that made me think a lot of people had probably told her just that.

I thanked her again and watched her drive off with her dream date. Then I bedded Orphan and walked home. Carl hadn't come by all day. I thought for sure he would have checked in to see how Orphan was doing. But he hadn't called. Maybe he hadn't cared.

~~~~~~~~~~~~~~~~~~~~~~~~~~~~~~

Monday after school Carl was waiting for me at the barn. "She looks so much better!" he called as I walked up.

I knew it was dumb for me to be mad at him for not coming by on Sunday, but I couldn't shake it. "I didn't know if you'd be by or not," I said, not looking at him. "I mean, when you didn't come back Saturday night or yesterday."

"I was here, Scoop," Carl said. "I looked in a couple of times. I saw Maggie and Jen here, and I kept my distance. And I saw the vet too."

So that was it. Still the same old secretive Carl.

Orphan really did look better. Carl helped me change her dressing, holding the cotton pad while I wound the bandage. When we finished and I led her up and down the stallway, she didn't limp at all.

"I think she'll be fine by tomorrow, Scoop," Carl said.

"Doc Snyder said it was okay to ride her when she stopped limping, but I don't know, Carl. I'm not taking any chances—not with Orphan. Not again."

"Then in the meantime," Carl said, "we'd better get back to the lessons."

"Huh?"

"Come with me, Scoop." Carl walked through Orphan's stall. "You're about to meet your new horse. True, he's a bit wooden, kind of rough. But he'll serve his purpose."

I followed Carl out across the paddock to the back fence. He had tied his English bridle to the top of a fence post, with the four reins hanging down. "Scoop," he said in a mock formal tone, "I'd like you to meet Wood-row, your new trusty steed. Mount up!"

For the next hour I practiced holding the four reins of the English bridle. It felt weird to use both hands and let the reins split my fingers.

"Hold your hands upright," Carl commanded. I might as well have been on a real horse, taking orders again. "Thumbs up! Feel it, Scoop," he said. "Remember. Curb rein on the bottom. Turn your thumbs toward Wood-row's neck, and the curb bit brings his head down. Back up, and you put pressure on the snaffle for signals to stop or slow down."

"I think Wood-row's got the stop command down already," I said.

But Carl was all business. "Bring your hands up higher over the withers. That's it."

I felt pretty stupid and could imagine what Stephen and his dad would say if they saw me. After a while, my hands felt stiff and my back ached. But I had to admit—the reins felt less awkward the longer we worked.

Carl and I practiced horseless on Tuesday and Wednesday. Even though Carl insisted Orphan was fine and even though I knew I needed the riding practice, I wanted to give Orphan an extra rest. We lunged her and led her. She played in the pasture and ran and rolled in the mud like normal.

~~~~~~~~~~~~~~~~~~~~~~~~~~~~~~

On Thursday after school Orphan herself was begging me to ride her. I jumped on her with nothing but a halter, and she took off to the pasture, where Carl was waiting for us.

"Finally!" Carl called to us as we trotted up bareback. "A real practice! You know that we only have one more practice after today, Scoop. So don't tell me you're not going to use the saddle today. Please?"

I sighed. It felt so wonderful to be sitting on Orphan, the wind blowing and trees whispering, and no leather separating me from my horse. But the show was Saturday. And if I didn't beat the Daltons at their own game ... I couldn't bear to even think about it.

I slid off, suddenly solemn. "Give me the saddle," I said.

This time the practice went so well I might have dreamed it. Orphan got every lead. I posted in time with Orphan's stride. We quit as soon as the first shadow struck the arena. One more practice to show time.

17

I still hadn't told Dotty about the horse show. Part of me wanted to, but I knew I'd never keep Carl a secret from Dotty. Besides, she'd been too busy all week finding the things Grandad squirreled away in the house. She didn't have time to worry about Orphan and me. First Grandad hid all the washcloths in B.C.'s closet. Then we found the forks in the laundry basket. It was like living in a magic show—things vanished.

But Friday morning, the day before the horse show, my stomach was too upset to eat the Hy-Klas cereal of the week.

"Dotty!" B.C. cried. "Scoop's not eating her Honey-Wheats."

I shot him a dirty look, but he didn't care.

Dotty sat down at the table with us and put her hand on my forehead. "Scoop, are you sick, Honey?"

I shook my head, but her hand never left my forehead.

Dotty removed her hand and stared straight

into my eyes, like she could see through to the other side. "Scoop?" She raised her eyebrows, but her eyes were so soft you could swim in them.

I caved. I couldn't hold it in any longer. "Tomorrow night I'm riding Orphan in the horse show."

B.C. dropped his spoon with a loud clank.

"I thought you didn't go in for that sort of thing," Dotty said. "I reckon this is about losing the barn?" She sighed, and the table wobbled when she let it out. "I tried every way I know how to come up with that money for you. Even asked Mr. Ford for a raise and an advance."

"Oh Dotty," I said, touching her arm. I knew how hard it would have been for her to ask. "I wasn't expecting you to come up with the money. That's why I'm entering the horse show. The Daltons are giving $500 to the winner of the English Pleasure Class."

"Cool!" B.C. said. "You and Orphan can beat anybody!" He was in one of his hyper moods and bounced in his chair, knocking the table with his knees.

I ruffled his hair, wishing I had his confidence. "I don't know, B.C. Stephen Dalton and Carla Buckingham are really good."

"Well," Dotty said, getting up from the table as Grandad shuffled out of B.C.'s old room. "We'll give this show to God. 'Cast your cares on the Lord.' Toss it up to Him, Scoop."

I forced a grin, wishing I could turn things over as quickly as Dotty could. But the show I was supposed to be tossing up felt like taffy stuck to my fingers.

~~~~~~~~~~~~~~~~~~~~~~~~~~~~

As soon as I stepped onto school grounds, Maggie ran up to meet me. "I'm sorry, Scoop! Don't be mad, please? I tried. I really did." She wore a French beret and a short, brown skirt. But she wasn't using an accent. "I didn't mean to, but I kind of let your secret slip to Jen. Are you mad?"

I waved to Jen, who was hanging back a few feet, probably waiting to see if I exploded. "It's okay, Jen," I called. She came closer. "I would have told you before now anyway, only Carl made me promise to keep him a secret."

"So," Maggie said, "tell! Does Carl think you and Orphan have a chance? I mean, I'm sure you do. It's just—"

"*We'd* vote for you," Jen said. "But will a judge?" She shifted the stack of books in her arms. "It's Orphan's first show. I can just imagine what Cheyenne would do with all that commotion."

"Well, there she is—the queen of the horse show circuit!" Stephen Dalton came strutting up to us. He knew!

I shot a dirty look to Maggie and Jen.

"I didn't tell anybody but Jen!" Maggie declared.

"I only told Travis," Jen said.

"Word's out you're a contender, Sarah Coop." Stephen's voice and smirk were mocking. "I'm shaking in my boots. Speaking of boots, do you even have any?"

Maggie stormed nose to nose with him, her hands on her hips. "Mock all you want, Stephen Dalton! Not only does she have boots, she has her own personal riding coach."

"Sure she does." He looked so smug.

"Well she does!" I could almost hear Maggie's blood sizzle. "Carl Buckingham's been coaching her with tips you couldn't even dream of!"

"Maggie!" I said.

Stephen turned to me. "A ghost for an instructor? That works. You've got about a ghost of a chance."

I wanted to wipe that smirk off his face. "He's not a ghost!" I yelled, not thinking, not listening to anything except my pride.

"If he's not a ghost—this great instructor of yours—" Stephen said, snot coming out of his nose as he snorted in disbelief, "how come nobody can ever see him except you?"

"You want to see him, Stephen?" I cried. "Do you really want to see him? Fine! We'll be in the south pasture tonight. Come and see for yourself!"

The minute the words were out I wanted them back. I'd broken my promise to Carl. And now he'd find out for sure. And after everything he was doing for me. How was I going to get out of this one? If Stephen Dalton took me up on my offer, what on earth was I going to do?

~~~~~~~~~~~~~~~~~~~~~~~~~~~~~~

Orphan whinnied as I neared her pasture for our last practice. I felt bad that I hadn't played with her much since we'd started practicing for the show. But she never held it against me. I'd never loved her more than when I watched her prance to meet me. The thought that she might not be there after Saturday weighed like a brick in the pit of my stomach.

When Orphan and I reached the arena, Carl was waiting. I felt a wave of relief. Stephen hadn't gotten to him yet at least. Carl held up a coat hanger with a plastic-wrapped black suit on it. "It's your riding habit," he said. "I'm pretty sure it will fit, but you better try it on tonight just in case."

I stared at it. "Carl," I muttered. "I know you said you'd take care of what I should wear, but I didn't expect this." A wave of regret passed through me when I remembered breaking my promise. Why had I told Stephen where we'd be? I glanced around the pasture, thankful to see nothing but grass and trees. Stephen probably didn't believe me anyway.

Carl handed me a black bowler helmet and a big box. I opened the box and could have fallen over with the scent of leather—shiny boots blacker than Orphan, without a scratch on them. "Are you sure it's okay to borrow this? It's not Carla's, is it?"

Carl gave me one of his scolding looks. I stuck my horsefeather into my jeans, saddled up Orphan, and we got to work. Orphan picked up her hooves higher and arched her neck royally. When we trotted, I forgot all about up, down, up, down, and moved with my horse.

"You two look great!" Carl hollered, after we'd run through every gait twice, reversed and run through them again. But I didn't need Carl to tell me we looked good. For the first time, I could picture riding Orphan in the show, having them call out my name as the winner.

"I want to quit now and give Orphan a good night's sleep," I said, not wanting to press my luck in case Stephen decided to pay us a visit. I patted Orphan's neck. She had barely worked up warmth under her mane.

"Okay," Carl said. "Let's meet at your barn at 8:00 A.M. I'll help you give Orphan a bath and braid her mane." He pulled a handful of red ribbons out of his pocket. "They match Orphan's bridle."

This was all getting too real. Something like little horseflies buzzed in my stomach. "So what time should we show up on the horse show grounds?"

"Since you'll have to ride Orphan over, plan to be there by 7:00. That will give her time to get used to everything."

"Can you ride over with me, Carl? Or, should we just meet there?"

Carl got quiet, and that storm cloud I'd seen before passed over his face. "I can't see you there, Scoop."

"Horsefeathers, Carl! You have to be there! I won't know what to do if you're not there. You don't even have to talk to me. You can signal or something."

I felt more and more desperate when he didn't say anything. "Carl, you can hide. Nobody even has to know you're there!"

Finally he said quietly, "I can't be there. That's all there is to it. I'll see you tomorrow morning at 8:00 for last-minute instructions. Don't ask me anything else. Remember our pact, your promise."

"It was a stupid promise! What's going on, Carl? Why are you like this?"

For a second it looked like Carl was going to say something. He put one hand on the bill of his Padres baseball cap and opened his mouth to speak.

Behind the hedgeapple trees came a sharp whinny. Orphan gave a long answering whinny and stamped her foot. Someone was coming. Carl and I looked up at the same time. A horse and rider appeared at the far end of the pasture.

"Scoop! Somebody's coming!" Carl jerked Ham's reins.

"Don't go, Carl!" I shouted. "He just wants to meet you."

Carl wheeled around on me. "You ... you told him about me? But you promised! Scoop," he whispered, "what have you done?" Then he jumped on Ham and rode away.

"Carl!" I yelled. "Come back! Please! I'll make them go away!" But it was too late. I knew he couldn't hear me. He'll be back, I told myself. Carl will get over being mad. Everything will be just like it was.

"So where's this Carl?" Stephen asked, pulling up Champion a few feet away. The gelding's flaxen mane and tail flowed in the wind like angel's hair.

I scooped up the riding habit and boots Carl had brought me and led Orphan out of the pasture, ignoring Stephen's taunts behind me.

~~~~~~~~~~~~~~~~~~~~~~~~~~~~~~~

That night over Spaghetti-O's I told the whole story to Dotty, B.C., and Grandad. "I think Carl will get over being mad though, don't you?" I asked when I'd finished the story.

B.C. shrugged, his mouth full of the Oreos we had for dessert. Grandad slipped a handful of the round, chocolate cookies into the pocket of his bathrobe.

Dotty said, "I hope so. You owe that boy an apology. Tell you what. Bring him home for supper."

I wondered what Carl would think of supper at our house, with Grandad swiping who-knows-what, B.C. likely to run off to the roof, and food served out of white Styrofoam cups priced with black markers.

"Can you come to the horse show tomorrow night?" I asked Dotty.

"Oh Honey, you know I promised Mr. Ford I'd work Saturday nights. It's overtime. We can use it. But I'll see what I can do. Could be I can slip away, okay?"

I carried my dishes to the sink and set them in the standing water. "Sure. Don't worry about it, Dotty." I watched the dishes sink into murky water and felt like I was sinking with them. Tomorrow night at this time I'd be prancing around the ring with a couple of dozen highbrow horses. And if I didn't win, it would probably be the last time I'd ever ride Orphan.

18

Saturday before it got light I headed for the barn and Orphan. I even got out of the house before Dotty. I fought the urge to think of everything as "the last time"—the last sunrise I'd greet with Orphan, the last ride, the last day I had any hope.

I brushed Orphan from the tip of her ears to the end of her fetlocks. No matter what happened, neither of our lives would be the same after tonight. I pulled out the horsefeather and stroked Orphan's chin with it. She stretched out her neck and closed her eyes.

I checked my watch. Ten minutes after 8:00. Carl hadn't shown. "Probably overslept," I told Orphan. "Don't you worry. He'll be here. He wouldn't bring us this far just to dump us the day of the horse show." But inside I was trembling. The air was thick and still and felt kind of like wet sand.

I waited another hour, hoping Carl would come. But in my heart, I knew better. I jogged back to the house to get shampoo and sponges and the ribbons Carl had left me. I wanted to call Maggie and Jen and get them to help me give Orphan a bath and braid her mane, but there was still a chance Carl might change his mind and show up. I didn't want to risk losing him again.

I had thought it would be fun getting ready for the horse show. I'd pictured Carl and me working on Orphan together. But it wasn't fun alone. Orphan didn't think so either. She didn't mind having her mane braided, but it took me over an hour before she'd let the hose anywhere near her. By the time I soaped and rinsed, braided and brushed, it was well into the afternoon.

I was brushing out her tail when I heard something behind me. "Carl?" I said, hope brushing against my heart.

B.C. stood just inside the barn, the sunlight bright behind him. He walked up and patted Orphan's shoulder. "Orphan looks different," he said.

"They all look like that for horse shows," I said, patting her rump, which shined and felt smooth as silk.

"I like the old Orphan better," B.C. said.

"What do you know?" I snapped. Then I was sorry I'd said it. I liked the regular Orphan better too. "Sorry, B.C.," I said. "I'm just edgy about the show. I don't know what I'll do if I lose Orphan."

"Maggie Magenta called you," B.C. said. "She talked funny—like those people did in that movie about bullfighters. So I'm not sure what she said, but I think she said, 'Long live backyard horses!' and 'See you at the horse show.'"

I smiled. It would be good to have Maggie there in any color.

B.C. turned to go.

"B.C.!" I called after him. "Pray for us, okay?"

B.C. left, and I did the best I could braiding Orphan's forelock, not knowing if I was supposed to or not. A minute later something clanged and scraped overhead. I knew it was B.C. settling in on the barn roof to have a talk with God. I buried my face in Orphan's neck and thanked God for B.C.

The afternoon dragged. About 4:00 I realized I hadn't eaten anything all day. I ran home and ate cold pork 'n' beans out of the can. B.C. was asleep on Dotty's bed, and I heard Grandad pacing in B.C.'s old room.

When I couldn't take it any longer, I put on the riding habit Carl had given me. I wished Dotty could have been there to tell me I didn't look as stupid as I felt. The only full-length mirror was on the outside of B.C.'s door. I tiptoed over to it.

The door swung open and I was staring face-to-face with Grandad. He squinted and studied

me up and down. "Horsefeathers! You look like
a penguin with boots on," he said in his gruff
voice.

"Thanks for the vote of confidence," I said,
trying to peer around him at the mirror. Everything fit okay, but the jacket was stiff and folded
every time I bent my elbow. The boots felt heavy,
and I heard a swishing sound when I walked.

Grandad shook his head at me. "Horsefeathers."

In that get-up, I had to walk slowly to the
barn to get Orphan. As soon as she saw me, she
stuck out her neck, showed her teeth, and
laughed.

"Oh yeah?" I said, scratching her chin. "You
look pretty ridiculous yourself, you know." I
pressed my face against her head and whispered,
"This is it, Girl."

I gave one last look around the barn, hoping
Carl would appear like a ghost out of thin air.
But he didn't. I'd broken my promise. And he'd
kept his—he wasn't going to come.

I'd scribbled a note for Carl before I left the
house: *Carl, I'm sorry I broke my promise. Please
don't let us down. I'll be looking for you at the horse
show.* I pulled the note from my pocket, and the
horsefeather fell to the ground. I picked it up
and ran the soft tip of the feather across my face.
Then, poking the feather's end into a crack, I
stuck the note up above Orphan's stall.

I saddled Orphan and rode off to the West Salem Horse Show. From a mile away, lights shone from the show grounds. A little closer I heard the horse show noises: a man's scratchy voice announcing something I couldn't make out, horns honking, a radio, horses talking back and forth, daring each other, challenging one another to battle.

Orphan stepped so high she was bouncing. "Don't be scared, Girl," I whispered, stroking her neck. I wished I could feel her under me and she could feel me. But the infernal saddle sat between us, separating us.

The first person I saw when we reached the horse show grounds was Mrs. Gopher. "Look at you! Aren't you adorable!" she raved.

Great. Just the look I was going for—adorable. "Hello, Mrs. Gopher."

"I knew Carla was riding, Carla Buckingham. And I knew Stephen always attends horse shows. I didn't know you had a horse."

"She doesn't," said a voice. I turned to see Stephen Dalton sitting on Champion. "You look ridiculous," he whispered so Mrs. Gopher couldn't hear. Stephen had on the same stupid riding habit I did. Everybody did. "Where did you get that saddle?"

"Carl loaned it to me," I said.

"Right, Carla's imaginary brother. Well, you might as well be riding an imaginary horse because you don't stand a chance. Where is the infamous *Carlos the Friendly Ghost* anyway?" Stephen stood in his stirrups and craned around to scan the crowd.

"Well, good luck to both of you," said Mrs. Gopher, walking off.

My stomach felt like boiling oatmeal. The last thing I needed was Stephen. I pivoted Orphan around and got out of there. We weaved in and out of trailers and trucks. A Shetland pony tied to a trailer switched his tail hard. I couldn't stand the terror I read in his eyes. Reaching down, I scratched his withers as we passed. He lifted his head and nickered.

Two girls not more than 7 or 8 years old, dressed exactly alike, rode by on two big palominos. Twins on twins. I thought about what Carl had said about feeling like two people. I looked around hoping to see Carl, but I knew he wouldn't be there.

"This is not the Indian princess I expected." Ray grinned up at me. It surprised me how glad I was to see him. "Have you seen Carla?" he asked.

"No." I couldn't have explained why it knocked the wind out of me to have Ray ask.

"Man, she might even beat Stephen," Ray said. "I don't know much about horses, but she looks awesome." He looked me up and down. "You sure you want to wear that get-up?"

"I *don't* want to wear it, but that's how it's done. I better get signed up and see when my class is."

"I'll be cheering for you and Orphan!" Ray called.

I got number 117 when I signed up for the English Pleasure Class. I sure hoped that didn't mean there were already 116 other people in the class. The lady at the registration table handed me four safety pins. "Have your mother or father pin the number on."

"I will," I said. "Thanks."

I looked around until I found Mrs. Gopher. She called me Sally once and stuck me with the pins twice. But she was really nice about helping me. And when she wished me luck, I could tell she meant it. Maybe I'd been wrong about her too. I made a mental note to stop calling her *The Gopher*.

There were four classes before mine. During each class, they announced the grand prize to be given away to the winner of the Pleasure Horse Class. As hot and uncomfortable as I was in that stupid riding habit, I could tell poor Orphan felt even worse in her stupid braids and English saddle. She stamped her foot and shook like she was shaking off extra water.

"After tonight I'll never make you wear it again, Orphan," I whispered. Then I thought about what I'd said. After tonight I probably wouldn't get a chance to make Orphan do anything again.

"Line up your horses for the final English Pleasure Horse Class!" The PA system echoed the words through the park, as if the wind carried them on purpose.

I gave Orphan a hug, and felt a shiver travel all the way through to my boots. There must have been about 20 horses in line ahead of me and maybe a dozen behind. Orphan and I kept dropping back farther and farther as horses pressed toward the gate.

I could smell fear sweat from the horses. Beside me an Arabian mare let out a squeal, a cry for help. The rider, a boy about B.C.'s age, looked as scared as the mare. "You might want to ease up on the reins," I said, reaching over and stroking the mare's shoulder. The boy loosened his grip on the reins, and the mare seemed to relax.

"Out of my way!" Stephen Dalton bumped past me on Champion. His boot brushed my leg and left a dirt print on my black jodhpurs. I wiped it off. When I looked up, Stephen was at the front of the line, with Carla a couple of horses back. Ray was right. She and Ham looked awesome. I couldn't see any way I could beat them.

19

All of a sudden the horses moved as if an invisible dam had burst and we were spilling over. Someone had opened the gates. The announcer shouted, "*Enter your horses at a trot!*"

Before I knew what happened, Orphan and I were trapped outside the gate in the back of the pack, while the other horses trotted halfway around the ring without us. I tried to squeeze my thighs and make contact through that stiff saddle to get Orphan to move. Finally we edged into the mainstream, one hat bobbing up and down in a sea of hats.

The sweaty smell of nervous horses mixed with dust and fresh manure. The lights were the brightest I'd ever ridden in. They made the horses blend together in shiny waves.

"*Walk your horses, please,*" came the voice of the ringmaster.

I hadn't even made it all the way around the ring. I couldn't see the ringmaster or the judge. Too many horses bunched together, with me squished to the rail and no room to move. Carl had warned me about getting trapped on the outside next to the rail where the judge would never notice me.

I tried to get to a free space between horses. I knew the canter would be called at any minute. I had almost made it to a good spot on the inside, when Stephen walked Champion right smack in front of me. They filled my spot and forced me to the rail again.

Somebody yelled, "Go Stephen and Champion!" I knew it was Stephen's dad, praising him for running me over.

"*Canter your horses!*" Cantering organ music, the William Tell Overture, blared over the speakers.

The thud of horses' hooves in the sawdust from every side made me feel as if I were in a buffalo stampede. Orphan took the correct lead on her own, favoring her left foot like Carl had instructed us. I wanted the judge to see how good Orphan was doing. I wished Carl could see too.

"Stay out of my way!" Stephen barked. "You don't belong here." He wouldn't budge, and neither would his horse. I was stuck next to the rail, completely blocked from the judge's view.

He's right. I don't belong here. I tried to push the thought from my head and get out of the trap that kept me hidden from the judge. But each time I cantered faster to get to a clearing, Stephen moved with me, blocking me off.

Then I saw Carla coming up on the inside. She and Ham flowed past Stephen, pulled in front of him, then slowed down. Orphan and I kept going at the same pace, and all of a sudden we were out in the open. Nothing stood between the judge and us. I felt him look at me as we cantered the length of the arena.

"Have fun, Scoop. You have to enjoy it." The words came from behind me, or I thought they did. But it sounded like Carl. I risked a glance back. Carla and Stephen were a length behind me. Maybe I'd imagined it.

Now that I was in the open, I could see the individual horses and riders. They all looked the same, straight-backed riders and high-stepping horses. The judge eyed them just as he had me. I felt my hopes draining out like sand in an hourglass.

The announcer called us to a walk. *"A big thanks goes to Dalton Stables for our grand prize. Five hundred dollars goes to the winner of the Pleasure Class!"*

Pleasure? I thought as I watched the circle of bowler hats bob up and down. There's no pleasure in this ring. Orphan was sweaty. Under her saddle, I sensed her back twitch.

The gate was closed now, but as I came around I spotted Maggie balancing on top of it. Jen and Ray were with her. They cheered as I rode by.

Orphan nickered. I felt sorry for her. It flashed back at me how I'd ridden her round and round that boring arena in the pasture when all she'd wanted was to run free, how I'd pushed and pushed until she'd gotten hurt. And now this.

"Scoop! There she is!" B.C. was waving with one hand and tugging at Grandad Coop with the other. "There's Scoop!"

"Horsefeathers!" growled Grandad. "That ain't Scoop. And that sure ain't Orphan."

I looked down at the red ribbons in Orphan's mane. The riding habit tugged at my neck until I thought I couldn't breathe. "Horsefeathers!" I said. "He's right! Orphan, this isn't us! You don't have to be like these fancy horses. And I don't have to be like Carla or Stephen."

I reached down and hugged Orphan. We were coming up on B.C. and Grandad again. I reined Orphan over to them and let the other horses pass me.

"What are you doing?" B.C. yelled.

Maggie, Jen, and Ray ran up to the arena. "Scoop?" Maggie squealed. "What's wrong?"

I hopped off Orphan, unbuckled the saddle, slid it off and threw it to them. "There! That's more like it." I whipped off my jacket and tossed it to B.C. Then I swung up on Orphan and rode bareback into the ring. "*Now* it's a pleasure class," I whispered to Orphan.

Orphan and I sailed among the other horses. They were mechanical, and we were flesh and blood. We were the ones who belonged, and I'd never felt closer to my horse than right then. My heart prayed, *Thank You, God, for making me just like You have, for making me belong to You in Your Son.* I could have sworn Orphan had wings as we floated through the mass of horses.

"Yea, Scoop!" I heard Dotty's voice before I caught sight of her waving at me with both arms.

"You made it!" I yelled as I soared past. We loped beside a Buckskin mare who refused to canter. Her rider, a girl about my age, kicked furiously, but the Buckskin only trotted faster. I leaned over and clicked at the mare, willing her to canter. She broke into a smooth gait right behind Orphan.

Once I heard Stephen's voice, "What do you think you're—" But Orphan and I were in a world of our own where Stephen couldn't touch us.

I passed Carla, and she smiled so big at me. I thought I'd seen that smile before, but Carla never smiled at school. Still ...

"*All right, riders. Bring in your horses and line them up.*"

I didn't even have to rein in Orphan. Without that saddle between us, she knew exactly what I wanted. We were the first ones in. Orphan stretched out straight, and I was more proud of her than I'd ever been.

A boy with a Tennessee Walking Horse I'd noticed getting long looks from the judge pulled up beside me. "Hey!" he shouted, and his horse bolted into Orphan. The boy dropped the reins, and the horse threw his head, preparing to rear. Without the saddle, I was free to slide off Orphan and pick up the dropped reins. "Shh-h," I said, scratching the horse's neck as I handed up the reins.

The kid moved his Walking Horse farther down the line, and I saw what his problem was. Stephen. I didn't know what Stephen had done, but he looked pretty pleased with himself. I swung up on Orphan's bare back.

"Couldn't you and that nag keep a saddle on? You look stupid. You're cluttering up the arena. Why don't you just leave now?" Stephen said every word out of the side of his mouth while looking straight ahead of him, a fake smile fixed to his face.

I glanced to my left and saw Carla and Ham looking shiny and perfect. I was sure Ham had gone through every gait without a fault. *Great. Carla on one side, Stephen on the other.*

Only then did I let myself admit there was no way I was going to win. They couldn't give a prize to Orphan and me. I wasn't sorry I'd taken the saddle off. Orphan wasn't like the other horses. Maybe that's why I loved her so much. Taking that saddle off was what she'd wanted me

to do. But now I'd have to face the conse-
quences. If it really happened, if I had to lose
Orphan, I just prayed that neither of us would
forget this night and that bareback ride of rides.

I glanced at Carla and was surprised at the
concerned look on her face. I wondered if maybe
Carl had been right and Carla wasn't as bad as
I'd made out. She'd definitely gotten Stephen
out of my way in the ring, although I had no way
of knowing if she'd done it on purpose.

"*We have a fine group of horses,*" bellowed
the ringmaster over the speakers. "*Let's give them
a hand.*"

I looked around the ring and found Dotty
with B.C. and Grandad. Next to them were
Maggie, Jen, and Ray, all clapping like crazy—for
me. The only thing that could have helped more
would have been to see Carl there.

"*Okay,*" said the announcer. "*We have the
winners.*"

The crowd got quiet.

"*In fifth place is Dantel Angeles on Califor-
nia's Mystic Dream!*" A little girl with braids
sticking out under her bowler hat trotted a dap-
ple gelding out of line and up to the judge's
stand to receive her pink ribbon.

"Hurry up, already!" Stephen griped.
"Three more losers before I get my trophy."

Neither Carla nor Stephen had been called
when they got down to announcing second

place. "*Second place goes to—Stephen Dalton!*"

"What?" Stephen screamed. "There must be some mistake!"

"*Mr. Stephen Dalton, please ride forward for your ribbon.*"

Stephen spurred his horse and galloped to the front, grabbed the ribbon and rode off, leaving dust in the judge's face.

"*First place in English Pleasure Class and the grand prize of $500 go to—*"

I closed my eyes and held my breath, the slightest trace of hope left, hoping to hear my name called.

"*Carla Buckingham!*"

I exhaled. The crowd applauded.

Instead of riding up for her trophy, Carla turned and stared straight at me. Then she pulled something out of her pocket. And just before she rode up, she stuck the horsefeather in her hat.

20

Horsefeathers!" I whispered, staring at the wisp of horsefeather stuck in Carla Buckinghams's hat.

Carla glanced back at me and slid her hat around backwards—just like all the baseball caps. And I knew. "Carl?" It had to be. The horsefeather. The backwards cap. The smile.

I stared stupidly at the back of that horsefeather as Carl ... or Carla ... or whoever ... rode toward the trophy stand. I squeezed my thighs into Orphan and galloped after them, ramming into the hind end of Ham. Carla pivoted in the saddle and shot me a scowl.

Only it was Carl. I couldn't believe I hadn't seen it before! Carla and Carl were the same person!

"You liar!" I screamed. "How could you do that? Some big joke on the hick orphan girl?"

Carla stammered something at me, spitting out words I couldn't make out.

The announcer cleared his throat over the speaker, then said something about the trophy winner and the grand prize.

"YOU! ... word ... Mar—" Carla was trying to say something that didn't make any sense. Orphan pranced alongside her, chomping at the bit. Out of the corner of my eye, I saw streaks of horses trotting past us, riders bobbing in a blur as the arena emptied.

Scenes from the past few weeks bumped in my head, trying to fit together. Carla and Carl were the same person! No wonder I could never see them together. Baggy clothes. Baseball caps. No wonder I was the only one dumb enough to fall for it. But why? Why would he ... *she* ... do it?

Again a voice scratched over the microphone, pleading for the winner to come and accept her trophy.

"Just a minute!" I shouted as Carla started to ride off. Horses were still parting around us, like river water around boulders. I pulled Orphan up beside Ham. "Why? Why did you make me think you had a twin brother?"

Carla stopped. Ham's head nudged Orphan, and Carla's face was so close to mine, I could see a film of dust under her eyes. "*You* thought that one up on your own!" she said.

"I did not!"

"You did too. I tripped, and you laughed at me. I was so nervous moving here, I ran back into the house. When I came out later to try to make friends, I found you and Orphan on the road. *You* thought I was a twin brother. I had my hair up in my cap. You called me Carl. I just went along with it. It's the only reason you gave me another chance. You already hated Carla. You were nice to Carl."

"But the boxes! They were marked Carl and Carla!"

"Carl—Carla? Sarah Coop—Scoop? I guess that makes you two people too."

I could have pushed her perfect, smug face in. "You should have told me. You let me go on believing you were Carl. Horsefeathers! I made an idiot out of myself at school. Me trying to convince everybody you were twins. And you let me do it!"

Carla looked away, then fumbled with some words I couldn't understand. For a minute I thought she wasn't going to answer. Finally she got it out. "You never would have been friends with Carla, would you? Admit it."

"*We're waiting for Carla Buckingham on Buckingham's British Pride. Will you please ...*" The announcer's voice drifted in the breeze over our heads, as if swallowed up by the lights that blurred the crowd. Only two people were left in that ring: Carla and me.

Carla's eyes got watery and spilled over and down her face. But her glare was as hard as ever. "Would you have met me every day after school if you'd known I was Carla?"

I didn't say anything, but I knew the answer. The organ music started up. The announcer was still pleading. I heard several voices yelling our names outside the ring, but they sounded like they were under waves of water.

Orphan and Ham stood still now. I felt my throat fill up as I stared at Carla. She was breathing in short, shaky spurts. I didn't think I could talk, even if I'd known what to say.

"Maybe I should have told you," Carla went on. "But you don't know what it's like! It's so hard for me to fit in! Doesn't matter where we move. I never ever belong there!"

Her voice was quivering, and I had to concentrate so hard to understand her, my head hurt.

She went on, repeating words three times when I couldn't get them. "Remember when we talked about being two different people? That's what I feel like most of the time! I can't talk like other kids or hear what they hear. But on a horse, in that pasture, when I was Carl, you acted like we were friends, like I belonged there. It was worth acting like two people."

"That doesn't make any sense, Carl— *Carla*," I said, correcting myself. I wanted to stay mad at her, to scream so I wouldn't cry. "*I'm* the one who doesn't belong. But you don't see *me* putting on a big show to make fools of everybody! I don't go around pretending I'm somebody else!"

Carla shook her head and said something I couldn't understand.

"Talk slower!" I shouted. "I can't understand a word you're saying!"

"See?" she shouted back at me.

"See what?" I said, trying to still Orphan, who was starting to get fidgety again.

Carla touched her hearing aids. "This! Half the time I can't hear what's going on. The other half I wish I couldn't hear because somebody's making fun of the way I talk!"

"That's not true," I said defensively, pushing out of my mind the time I'd laughed on the inside, right along with Stephen.

She opened her mouth then stopped as suddenly as if she were a trumpet and whoever was blowing her ran plumb out of air. Then I think she whispered to Ham, "What's the use ...?" When she lifted her head, Carla had muddy splotches running down her face.

Ham and Orphan had moved so close together, Carla and I were almost bumping noses. I couldn't stop staring at her, even when I heard people coming out for us. One minute she looked like Carl had in the pasture. The next minute she looked like Carla.

Lord, help me understand, I prayed. Then something inside me unfolded, like my room unfolding itself at night. And I felt as if Carla were my own sister, as if we belonged to the same family and I didn't want to lose her too. "Carla," I said, "I'm sorry. Can you—"

But before I could finish, Ham jerked her away. "What on earth are you doing, Carla?" It was Carla's mother, dressed in a navy business suit, her hair pulled back in a barrette. She had Ham's reins and was leading him toward the trophy stand.

"*Here comes our winner now! That's Carla Buckingham on Buckingham's British Pride! They're really coming!*" shouted the announcer, sounding like he just woke up. But he didn't get any applause. The crowd had already wandered off.

I watched them walk away, Carla's horse-feather still stuck crooked in her backwards bowler. Only then did the full force of my defeat hit me. Monday morning the bank note came due. The lease would be signed over to Dalton Stables. Everything would be lost—including Orphan.

21

Dotty and everybody rushed into the arena and tried their best to make me feel better. Ray even walked Grandad home so Dotty and B.C. could walk with Orphan and me to the barn. Once I had Orphan cooled down and brushed, I knew there was no way I was leaving her that night. When I asked Dotty if I could spend the night in the barn, she didn't say a word. She just pulled down an old horse blanket and tossed it to me. Then she and B.C. left me with the best horse in the whole world.

~~~~~~~~~~~~~~~~~~~~~~~~~~~~~~

I woke to Orphan's soft nickering, my head on her neck. For a minute I thought I was still dreaming. I was in Orphan's stall under a faded green horse blanket.

Orphan whinnied, then got to her feet. All I could think was that they were coming to take her away. I got up and clung to her firm, sleek neck. She stretched out her head and rested it on my shoulder. Then I heard something coming from the pasture.

I peered out of the open stall door. The sun was coming up, shining an orange light on a group of people and horses as they made their way through the pasture.

I heard Maggie's laugh first. She was standing on the back of her white horse. Cheyenne, Jen's Paint, was there. And as they got closer, I saw that Travis was leading Cheyenne and Jen was sitting on her. Behind them followed a slew of little Zuckers, each carrying something—a paint brush, a bucket, a broom.

Orphan and I stepped outside. I watched in amazement as the noisy crowd came closer, tramping on dewy grass that sparkled in the sunlight. Grandad, Dotty, and B.C. brought up the rear. And leading the parade was Carla Buckingham on her prancing bay. Carla was grinning her Carl grin.

Maggie trotted up to me, lifted her reins, and Moby bowed deeply. "Isn't this just the best!"

"What's going on, Maggie?" I asked as I took in more and more of the scene—B.C. with a hammer, Grandad carrying a bag of carrots, Ray with a rake.

Dotty ran up and hugged me breathless. Her tears gathered in the bags under her eyes. "Our phone rang off the hook last night, Scoop! It was like everybody got the same idea all at the same time." She turned to Carla and Ham. "Carla called first."

Carla slid off Ham. "You've taught me a lot about talking to horses, Scoop. And last night when I was chatting with Ham, he told me he's not happy at Dalton Stables. He wants to move in with Orphan. What he really wants is to be a backyard horse."

"But he can't stay here," I said, wide awake now but more confused than ever. "I lost. We lost the barn." I glanced at everybody. "You were all there at the horse show. You know I didn't win."

Mr. Zucker, a toddler in each arm, joined Dotty and shook his head. "We were there, Scoop. And what I saw at that horse show convinced me of what I knew all along. You have an amazing way with horses. A gift! I watched you calming other people's horses in that ring. That's when it hit me."

Mrs. Zucker broke in. "I told Mr. Zucker we should have thought of it months ago!"

I looked to Jen for help. I still couldn't get hold of what was happening.

"It's your dream, Scoop," Jen said. "A stable where horses are free to be horses." Cheyenne bolted, startled by something we couldn't see. Jen grabbed her saddle horn to stay on.

Travis had to dodge to keep from getting run over. "We're begging you to take on this beast, Scoop!" he said, scurrying out of the way of Cheyenne's hooves. "Tame her for us. Believe me! Whatever it costs to break her, it's worth it!"

"Not *break* her, Travis," Jen said, two hands still wrapped around the saddle horn. "*Gentle* her. You saw Scoop at work last night. You said she was a real horse whisperer and if you were a horse, you'd refuse to be tamed by anyone else."

I think Travis blushed, and I know I did. "I'd love to work with Cheyenne. But there's still the bank and the Daltons—"

Mrs. Zucker whipped a check from her husband's shirt pocket and shoved it at me. "We Zuckers always pay in advance," she said. "That's for Cheyenne's first month at your home for backyard horses."

"I can't take this," I said, feeling a lump in my throat.

"Please!" said Mr. Zucker. "It's not a gift. We watched you at that horse show. Even other people's horses calmed down when you rode near them. There's no one else I'd trust with Cheyenne."

"And Moby gets to come too!" Maggie squealed. "You should have seen me with Mother! It was my best dramatic role ever. She wanted Moby to go to Dalton Stables, but her fiancé—you know, Mr. Chesley—helped me convince her to let Moby come here. He was standing by the gate last night and saw you help some little boy and his horse. And he thought you were the best rider there! He's paying you what he would have paid the Dalton gang!"

I was afraid to blink, afraid I'd wake up from the best dream I'd ever had. I looked at Dotty, my eyes blurry. She threw her arms around me, knocking the horse blanket from my shoulders. "Scoop, with this money from your first three boarders, plus your savings and mine, we can pay off the bank."

Dotty stepped back, her hands on my shoulders, and stared into my eyes. "You'll have your work cut out for you, Hon. It won't be easy to turn this here barn into that backyard stable you've always dreamed about."

"I'll help!" cried B.C.

"How will you help, you little bottle cap?" Ray teased.

B.C. held up his hammer. "I'll work on the roof!"

Ray laughed. "And I'll help too. Just don't expect me to shovel manure. Anything but that."

"Anything?" Carla asked, grinning at him so that he probably *would* have agreed to anything.

"See?" Maggie said. "We'll board horses and you'll gentle them. I can teach them tricks that will astound their owners."

"We'll use my mash and feed," Jen said. "Horses will always leave in better shape than they came. Maybe we can even sell my fly spray.

Who knows?"

"Hey," Carla said. "I know a guy named Carl who could give riding lessons if you needed him to."

"You mean we get to keep everything?" I asked. I felt like I might burst into pieces right there.

"Now aren't you glad we gave everything over to God, Scoop?" Dotty said. "Just look at what He's done with it." She waved her hand toward the crowd behind her, all of them standing right there for me. I didn't share a drop of blood with any one of them, but we were all part of the same family.

Thanks, God, I prayed. I don't even know if I said it in my heart or whispered it out loud. I could have screamed it at the top of my lungs if the words hadn't been stuck in my throat.

I needed to hug somebody. B.C. was pulling with all his might on Grandad, who stubbornly hung back like a balky Shetland. I reached out and gave Grandad a hug.

"So what will you call your horse business?" B.C. asked.

"Horsefeathers!" Grandad muttered, shaking loose from my hug.

"You're right again, Grandad!" I said. "We'll call ourselves *Horsefeathers!*"

Carla pulled the horsefeather out of Ham's bridle and stuck it in Orphan's halter. "I think this belongs to you," she said.

Belongs. It was a good word. Carla was right. As I looked from face to face, I knew that I'd found a place where I belonged. "Come on in," I said, motioning them to the barn. "Welcome to Horsefeathers!"

Parts of a Horse

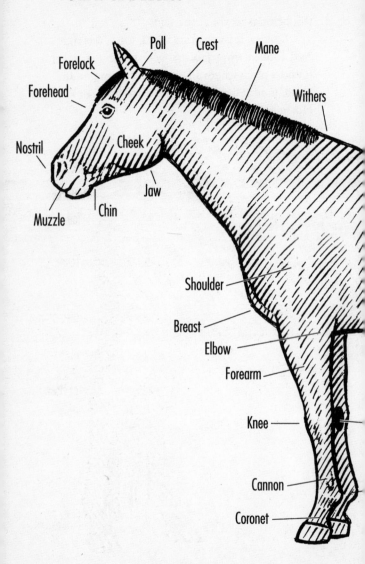

Poll
Crest
Mane
Forelock
Forehead
Withers
Nostril
Cheek
Jaw
Muzzle
Chin
Shoulder
Breast
Elbow
Forearm
Knee
Cannon
Coronet

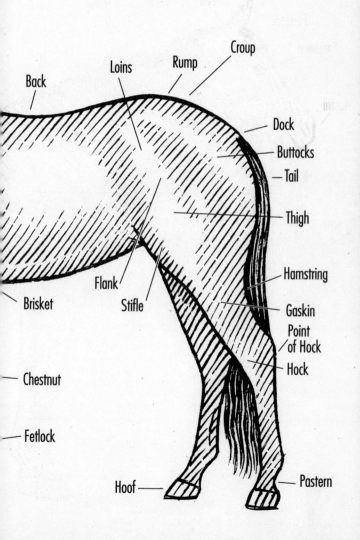

Photo by Brad Ruebensaal

About the Author

Dandi Daley Mackall rode her first horse—bareback—when she was 3. She's been riding ever since. She claims some of her best friends have been horses she and her family have owned: mixed-breeds, quarter horses, American Saddle Horses, Appaloosas, Pintos, and Paints.

When she isn't riding, Dandi is writing. She has published more than 200 books for children and adults, including *The Cinnamon Lake Mysteries* and *The Puzzle Club Mysteries*, both for Concordia. Dandi has written for *Western Horseman* and other magazines as well. She lives in rural Ohio, where she rides the trails with her husband Joe (also a writer), children Jen, Katy, and Dan, and the real Moby and Cheyenne (pictured above).